CRITICAL ACCLAIM FOR
NATHAN SINGER

"Nathan Singer's *The Duplication House* is at once a gleefully transgressive psychosexual phantasmagoria of Grand Guignol grotesqueries and a gimlet-eyed postmodern rumination on the creative process. Take a peek inside—I double-dare you."
—Chris Holm, Anthony Award winning author of
The Killing Kind and *Child Zero*

"The hip new grand master of America's literate underbelly."
—Mike Magnuson, author of *The Right Man for the Job*

"The master of the literary pulp thriller. Singer's work has beauty and brutality in a balance no other writer can match."
—Steve Weddle, author of *Country Hardball*

"Nathan Singer is an urban wordsmith that blisters the pages with language only he can scribe."
—Frank Bill, author of *The Savage*

"He's the kind of writer who'll just destroy you, in all the right ways."
—Benjamin Whitmer, author of *Cry Father*

THE DUPLICATION HOUSE

BOOKS BY NATHAN SINGER

A Prayer for Dawn
Chasing the Wolf
In the Light of You
The Song in the Squall
Transorbital
Blackchurch Furnace
The Duplication House

NATHAN SINGER

THE DUPLICATION HOUSE

Down & Out Books
3959 Van Dyke Road, Suite 265
Lutz, FL 33558
DownAndOutBooks.com

Cover design by JT Lindroos

ISBN: 1-64396-336-8
ISBN-13: 978-1-64396-336-5

For Karsten

All writing is pigshit.
—Antonin Artaud

"So...*when they found* my sister in the woods, she was naked, screaming, and drenched in blood. It wasn't her blood."

Thursday: 11am. Los Angeles

Drinking Jack Daniel's in Malibu Al's Beach Bar at LAX reading Dostoevsky's *Notes from the Underground.* "Tell it to me straight, Sal," I asked my agent, "does this make me less of an asshole than everybody playing Angry Birds on their phones, or more?" I was glad that he called. It had not been a great week up to that point. "I'm thinking more." A phone call from your lit agent is typically a positive thing, you know? "Quite a bit more, I'd wager." A check-in is probably just going to come via email. But a phone call? That is hot action, potentially. Forward momentum.

"You wanna maybe sober up a bit and call me back?" he replied. "It is two in the afternoon."

"Two New York time, Sally. It's breakfast at LAX."

"Of course."

"Sat behind Henry Winkler on the flight in."

"Oh yeah? The Fonz himself."

"I was going to tell him I loved him in *An American Christmas Carol*, but thought better of it."

"Good call."

"First row of coach. Wedged between two crabby old men. One kept injecting himself with...insulin? I'm assuming it was insulin."

"Living the dream, my friend."

The other had his face buried in a novel written by a buddy

of mine, currently holding the number one spot on the *New York Times* bestseller list. I considered telling the old timer I that knew the author, and that our debut novels had come out the same year. We had even talked about collabing on something at one point, my successful friend and me. But these old cats were clearly not about the yakkety yak yak. *Suits me just fine.* Instead, I spent the flight reading *Notes from the Underground* and making faces at a baby across the aisle. (Serendipity alert: looked up from the book at one point and noticed that the kid in the in-flight movie, *Life of Pi,* was also reading Dostoevsky.) The baby was three months old, maybe? She laughed and laughed.

"Thanks for entertaining her!" the mom said.

"I'm like a giant Muppet," I replied. I think the baby's dad was jealous. He kept kissing her, but she ignored him. *Sorry, bro. Don't hate the player, hate the game.*

"How did the pitch go?" Sal asked me. "Does Marsha seem hopeful at all? I downed the last of my Jack and ordered another. The day before I left, I had sold $70 worth of textbooks. Malibu Al's took the bulk of it. Damn you, Malibu Al! You go straight to Hell! "It was a disaster," I said. "The studio exec we met with was the same cat we had met eight years ago. Seriously, the same exact dude. He clearly did not remember me or my script, which I thought might be good news at first. But he spent the whole time talking about how rich he was, again, and how he had just bought a mountain chalet for his grandkids, and I had to sit there grinning and nodding like a simp. And then he passed on it. Again."

"Shit."

"Marsha said that this was the last shot. There is nothing more she can do."

It had been years of nearlys, almosts, and lottanothings. She was done with it, and rightly so.

"Sorry man," he said. "I'm sorry to hear it. It's a great script; you know that. Just probably not...you know...*commercial*, right?"

"I've got friends winning awards, Sal," I said. "Edgars, Grammys, Emmys, goddamn Oscars. *New York Times* bestsellers. Meanwhile, I can't even make rent selling plasma."

"No offense, brother, but I wouldn't buy your plasma."

"None taken."

I got really good reviews early on, you know. Lots of buzz about "the voice of a new literary generation," and whatnot. But reviews do not move units. Not always. I don't know what does. If I did, I probably wouldn't be sitting here about to yack my guts up in an airport bathroom before flying back to my roach-infested hovel in Ohio.

"It's a tough business."

I wouldn't be broke...

"For sure."

I wouldn't be buried in debt...

"You have to be willing to sacrifice a part of yourself."

"Too true." *Or all of yourself.*

"Since you're out there, did you see—"

"No," I said, cutting him off before he could say her name. "I did not see."

I wouldn't be ready and eager to snatch up any shit gig that oozes down the pike.

"You guys ended badly, huh? It has been some time now."

I'd probably still have a bad liver, though.

"No, we ended fine," I said. "Friends. Good terms. All that. But we were both still small potatoes when we separated. You know? Now she's got a pilot that is one final step from pickup, and she doesn't want to talk to me anymore because, now that I'm officially dead on the West Coast, she thinks I'm just going to try to, you know, sweet talk her into connecting me with her team."

"Which is true."

"Which is entirely true." That last drink started to hit me. I felt as if accusing eyes were upon me from a distance (or was it a camera lens?). I ordered a screwdriver, for the vitamins. "Did you hear, Sally? I am going back to school. Gonna get that degree."

"Another one?"

"Yeah."

"How does it feel, as a published author, to be sitting in a Creative Writing class with a bunch of kids?"

"Not super great."

"Do your fellow students know who you are at least?"

I had to laugh. "Who I am? Who *am* I?"

I'm the night prowler, get outta my way.

"Did you get grants?"

"Loans."

Sal exhaled deeply. "So…" he said, "you should probably maybe take this gig, yeah?"

This was not the first time I had been offered a gun-for-hire ghost writing job. Some years ago, I was hired to write a memoir for a young Filipino gentleman who had been held captive by militants in Iraq for eight brutal, harrowing months. He was starved, beaten, and kept in a dirt hole under a house for the entire length of time. Every day he was sure they would drag out him of the hole and kill him, or he would be left forgotten there to starve to death. Somehow, he never gave up hope, and his young bride back in the Philippines never gave up in her quest for his freedom. Finally, they got him out and home. It was an amazing, terrifying, uplifting true story of faith, love, hope and the triumph of the human spirit…

"What's the guy's name?" I asked.

So why did you never hear of this gripping, powerful work of narrative non-fiction?

"Seth Conlin."

Because it was never published. For the two years and change that my agent at the time (pre-Sal) shopped it, ALL the publishers, large and small, said "Great story. Loved it. So moving. Too bad he isn't American. Americans won't buy a book that isn't about an American." We were all flabbergasted. *That can't possibly be true!* we thought. The attitude was basically, "Yeah, sorry, we know that sounds racist/xenophobic, but this is a business. If we don't think it will sell, there is no point in us investing in it." Needless to say, I never got paid for the work.

"Seth Conlin," I repeated back.

"It's not about him, though. You wouldn't really be dealing with him. It's about his sister, actually. Emily, I think her name is."

"She was the missing person?"

"For sixteen years."

"She was officially classified a missing person by the FBI?"

"That is what I'm assuming."

"Never presumed dead?" I asked.

"I don't really know. You'll have to talk to them about that. I told you what he told me."

"That after sixteen years, his missing sister was found naked in the forest near their childhood home caked in blood."

"Not her own."

"That is a nice touch."

"Yeah," Sal replied with a raspy chuckle. "He thought you might like that." Pause. "He's a fan."

"You don't say," I said, crunching ice cubes. *Don't have many of those.*

"His sister, she's been staying with him. Their folks both passed on while she was missing. It seems that she has never really given much of a statement, due to the trauma, I guess. Police have pretty much given up. Apparently, though, the pair of them have been talking about some kind of a way for her to tell her story. To get it out to the world. When she's ready, of course."

"I get it."

"So, one night, she's up late with insomnia just grabbing books from his shelves to read, and she stumbles upon yours."

"Serendipitously enough."

"'He's the one,' she told Seth."

I had to laugh. "Yeah, okay."

"That's what he told me. So he rang me up."

"Huh. Which book?"

"I don't know; the gruesome one."

"That's funny, Sal."

"Do you want me to connect you and him? You can take it from there. Just let me know if we need to write up contracts and everything."

"What do you think? What should I do?"

"That is entirely your call, man."

"Are we actually gonna sell this one, Sally? Or is it just another spec in the wilderness?"

"You don't have to take it."

"Yeah…"

"I am thinking, though…"

"Yeah?"

"This guy Conlin, he owns his own business. I think he's doing pretty all right, all things considered. Young fella too. We could insist on a flat up front, then negotiate a royalty split after we find a publisher, god willing."

"And the creek don't rise."

"As they say."

"If I do take it, if I take this thing on, where am I heading?"

"West Virginia."

Jesus fucking Christ…

"I can't wait."

THE DUPLICATION HOUSE: DOORWAY

Wheeling

I met Seth Conlin at a little neighborhood bar on Warwood Ave. just outside of Wheeling, West Virginia. I had meant to look up his photo on his company's website prior to the meeting so I would know who to look for. It slipped my mind. Fortunately, he spotted me. As I stood awkwardly in the doorway, I saw a handsome, clean-cut young gentleman in designer jeans and polished, silver-tipped cowboy boots walking toward me grinning real big, holding two drinks. I regretted my slovenly, disheveled visage just then.

"Jack on the rocks, right?" he said, handing me a tumbler.

"Mr. Conlin, I presume." We clinked glasses, and he led me over to a booth in the corner.

"I really appreciate you making the trip," he said as we sat down.

"Nothing of it. Glad to be here."

"Did I get the drink right? I remembered that your protagonists frequently drink Jack on the rocks. Figured it must be a favorite of yours."

I smiled, genuinely flattered. "Yeah, it's great, thank you. My agent did tell me you are at least somewhat familiar with my work already."

"I've read 'em all!" he said, a bit more eagerly than I think he meant to, because he quickly dialed it back. "Or, I've read several of them. I don't know what all is out there."

"There are quite a few out of print, alas. Maybe we will have a new one for you before too long, though, yeah?"

Seth gave a bit of a half-smile and a small shrug. "Yeah, I might skip this one. No offense. It is a bit different now. Cuz it's my sister, you understand."

"Sure thing."

"You hungry? My treat. The food here is pretty basic, but it tastes good enough and there is plenty of it. I'll throw down a coupla bills on a meatball sub if you've got a hankering."

"Or..." I said, giving the menu a glance, "a deep-fried hot dog for a buck seventy-five. On a first date? Damn, I don't know if I can handle the pressure of expectation."

Seth laughed really hard at that. I laughed too, mostly at his laughing. In the moment, I got the sense that he probably hadn't really laughed in a while.

"No pressure, man, no pressure," he said, wiping his eyes on a paper napkin.

"I appreciate it," I said, raising my glass, "but just fluids, the doctor ordered."

"Let me know if you change your mind."

"Will do."

"You have been down this way before, correct?"

"Yep, once."

"I was tickled to see Wheeling pop up in one of your novels."

"Yeah," I chuckled. "My agent, Sal, the guy you talked to? He fucking *hates* that book."

"Really? Shit, I loved it!"

"Thanks. Well, you remember the psycho character in that one? The guy who tries to strangle the two priests—"

"With piano wire?"

"That would be the one. I thought, seeing as Mr. Willis is a devout Catholic and all, it would be hilarious to name that particular character after him. He... did not find it funny." We laughed. "I mean, he shopped it. But he was pissed."

"At least you changed the last name!"

"Right, but how many Salvadores do you know?"

"Fair point."

"So, speaking of," I said, downing my drink. Seth signaled to the bartender for another round. "I hate to be drab and official right from the get-go, and I don't know what Mr. Willis has told you about this sort of thing, but my standard flat is $7,500 up front, which, believe me, is insanely cheap. Sal would shop it, of course. In the event of a sale, fingers crossed, we split the advance in half. All royalties are 60/40. I have an okay relationship with a couple of publishers right now, and if one of them picks it up, we'll need to renegotiate a separate contract on e-sales and audio recordings, should you even decide to go with the latter. The former is a given, of course."

"Yeah, okay," Seth said with a shrug. He shrugged a lot. "That all sounds totally fine to me. Maybe a little too cheap, honestly, from what I've read. But y'all know your business better than I do. I'll cut you a check right now if you like."

"No, that's not necessary."

"You haven't even met Emily yet. You might change your mind. I wouldn't blame you if you did."

For reasons I still cannot fully make sense of, hearing him say her name out loud gave me a slight shudder. It was as if he had mentioned a ghost in passing. But he hadn't. She wasn't. I knew that. I had made the trip specifically to meet her.

A waitress brought over our drinks. "Y'all eatin'?" she asked.

Seth pointed finger guns at me. "Fried dogs?" he asked, his blue eyes twinkling.

"Who could say no?" I replied.

"Two dogs comin' up," she said, and departed.

"Driving in," I said, "I think every other billboard I saw said *Coal is Patriotic* or some such. Is that, like, the state motto?"

Seth sighed and shook his head. "Either that, or *Abortion Stops a Beating Heart.*"

"Oh yeah, that was a hot one too."

"Goddamn coal has got our nuts in a vise down here. Coal and Jesus."

"Coal and Jesus," I said. "I have all their albums."

13

"Hey, we've got whitewater rafting too!"

"But here's the thing, Seth," I said. "Closer and closer to Wheeling I got, the more I saw *Conlin Landscaping* billboards. Almost as many as the *Jesus Loves Coal* signs. I would be lying if I said I wasn't impressed."

Seth grinned. He had very pretty teeth. "We do okay. We do okay. Did you hear our radio spots? They're brand new as of this week."

"Only thing I heard on the local radio coming in was that an entire truckload of Phenobarbital has gone missing. Authorities are flummoxed."

"Good ol' Wes' Virginny!" he said, holding his beverage aloft. I did as well.

"*Saluté.*" We drank. "The Conlins have pretty deep roots in these parts, yeah? Original settlers maybe?"

"Couldn't really tell ya," Seth said, licking the gin from his bottom lip. "Mama never said a whole lot about the family tree. Em and me, we didn't really know our dad. I didn't know him at all. He and Mama split when Emily was ten and I was two. I remember meeting him, maybe once, but it might not even be a real memory. He moved to Knoxville, Tennessee and that was that. Drove a big rig. Got killed out there on the road, and Mama got a chunk of money from it. Mama passed when I was still in college, about six years ago."

"I'm sorry to hear that."

"It was hard, you know. It was real hard. I was all alone out here, pretty much still just a kid. But I inherited the nest egg and the house. Sold the house, used the money to start the business."

"Still alone now? I mean until recently."

"Like everybody else, I had dreamed about starting up a family someday. But the company has been my whole life, to be frank." Pause. "What about you? I noticed you dedicated your last book to some girl."

"Heh, yeah. No, we're not together anymore."

"Kids?"

"None that I've met so far."

"I hear ya. I've got a girlfriend, but we're just casual, you understand. I kinda like not having to be responsible for anyone. Anyone else. But...now I've got Em."

"Now you've got Em."

"Which is great, don't get me wrong. It's amazing to have her back in my life again after all this time. It's just...it's wild, I'll tell you what."

"Where is Emily now?"

"I stay here in town during the week, close to the office. But I've got a cabin out on Rock Lake about an hour and a half from here. Nine acres, right on the waterfront, no neighbors. Peace and quiet. That's where Em has been staying at for now. Downtown Wheeling ain't exactly Cairo, right, but it's still a bit too hustle-bustle for her just yet."

"And where are we now in relation to where she was found?"

"Three hours," he said immediately, as if he had been waiting for the question. "Nearly to the minute."

"Close to where you grew up, right? She was found near your hometown?"

"Barely even a town really. I don't exactly know what you'd call it. It's sort of close to Burlington, which is a pretty small town in its own right. Less than 200 people. Our town, or whatever, it's even smaller. It doesn't even have a name, to tell the truth of it. We usually refer to it as either near-Burlington, or Down Pattersons, cuz it's south of Route 50, just down Pattersons Creek."

"And that's where she vanished sixteen years ago?"

"No. No, it wasn't sixteen years. It was twenty years."

"So, she vanished near your town, turned up twenty years later screaming in the woods near that same town—"

"She wasn't screaming. She couldn't scream. They found her staggering through the brush with her mouth wide open, trying like hell to scream. But not so much as a squeak could come out." His voice began to falter. "She didn't make a sound for weeks.

15

And… sh-she was… she was…"

"I know. You don't have to say it."

"It's just hard."

"I'm sure."

"It is really fuckin' hard."

"And the whole time nobody knew where she was?"

"Oh…" Seth said, small. He looked down at his drink. The fingers on his left hand drummed against the table. "Oh, no. I knew exactly where she was."

At that moment, my throat went dry. I dropped an ice cube into my mouth, but it did not help at all.

"I beg your pardon?"

"I was with her when she disappeared."

My skin began to crawl.

"Um…what…what are you saying to me right now, Seth?"

He looked up at me, his lips shut. The flesh at the corners of his beautiful sky-blue eyes pinched tight.

Just then, the waitress arrived. "Here's your deep-fried dogs, fellas!" she chirped. Quickly sensing the tension at the table, she slid the plates in front of us gently, and stepped back. "I'll be over to check on y'all in a bit. Enjoy."

I picked up my hot dog and began to eat. Seth did not. *Nice. Hot mustard and spicy relish.* "I'm here for a job, Mr. Conlin. I'm here to tell a story. What sort of story are we telling here?"

"You need to talk to Emily," he whispered desperately, his voice and fingers trembling. "*It's not my story.*"

The House at Rock Lake

For an hour and a half, I followed Seth's taillights through the black of the West Virginia night. He gave me the address so I could GPS it, but he was correct when he told me it would try to take me to paths both ill-advised and impossible, down roads that have not actually been roads in quite a while.

The broken lines of the divider blipped by like an EKG. I tried to keep my eyes from succumbing to highway hypnosis. I thought about my last day in Cali before this venture...

I had decided to drive out to Palo Alto to visit Stanford University. I had always wanted to see it but had never been before. Loved it. It is unlike any other campus I had ever seen. There was something about seeing Guadalupe palms and avocado trees on a college campus that kind of blew my mind. I spent most of the afternoon walking the grounds, checking out the buildings. I had lunch at their bookstore café, chatted with some prospective students and their parents. It was cool. In another life, if I were someone different, I would have liked to have attended there. In another life, if I were someone different, I would have liked to teach there, maybe. But institutions like Stanford, like so many others, are designed to keep barbarians like me outside the gate. It is kind of like when colleges and prep schools will decide to teach one of my books in their "Contemporary Literature" courses. Occasionally, they will fly me out as some sort of exhibit for their students to gawk at. While I sit there dumb like a misplaced houseplant, they will examine and interpret my work like it's outsider art. Like finger-paintings of the insane. But they would never in 1,000 lifetimes let someone like me teach there. It is wild that my work is taught at schools I could never have attended. Probably couldn't get hired as a janitor, let alone faculty. But fuck it; a stipend is a stipend. And there are usually a few free meals involved. I don't know what I would do with that sort of consistent money anyway. Probably blow it all on rare texts and cocaine.

On the way back to my hotel, I stopped in at an interesting looking used book shop. As I walked through the door, page dust and the aroma of decaying wood pulp caressed my olfactory senses. *Intoxicating.* The young cat at the counter studied his phone intently. There were no other customers.

"Just you today?" I asked.

"I don't know how I'll manage," he replied, deadpan.

"You go to school at Stanford?"

He looked up at me incredulously.

"You serious, bro? They wouldn't even let me sweep up at that joint."

I nodded. "*Hermano,*" I said. He held up a fist of solidarity. Then he returned to his screen.

I had not been looking for anything specific, which was good, because there didn't seem to be any particular rhyme or reason for how their shelves were organized. There was literally a three-foot pile of $1 mass market paperbacks. Not a bin, not a box, just a loose pile. Somehow, I did spot a used, hardcover copy of my second novel shelved alongside what appeared to be a series of Mediterranean cookbooks.

"Yo, you want me to sign this?" I asked.

"Yeah, I guess," the kid replied. "Whatever."

I flipped to the title page to discover that I had, apparently, already signed it at some point. "*To Cindy,*" former me had written, "*Keep Art Dangerous.*"

Bleeeeeeeeeeeeeeeeeeeeeeeeccccccccchhhhhhhhh...

I had zero memory of writing that (though I must have recently been reading Edwidge Danticat). And I wondered if Cindy had heeded my advice, whoever she was. One thing is for certain; twenty-seven-year-old me could certainly have used a good slapping.

"Well, this is goddamn embarrassing," I said. "I think I should throw myself in front of a bus."

"Yeah, probably," the kid agreed, eyes still glued to his phone. "Wouldn't do much good, though. Lousy pedestrian-right-of-way law."

I ended up buying *Mother Night* for $2.75, one of the few Kurt Vonnegut books I did not already own.

There was nothing interesting going on around the hotel. There weren't even any bars nearby, which was probably good since I was nearly out of money, anyway. I spent the last of it on a bottle of Wild Turkey, a nickel of smoke, and a tube of toothpaste. I had to get a full-size tube because the store did not have the travel size, which sucked because I knew I was going to have to throw it away before I got on the plane the next day. Such a waste. (I bought the smoke off some young dude in the parking lot in a burgundy El Camino. He had one eye that didn't move and a huge gash in his cheek that did not appear to be fully healed. I would bet there is quite a story there).

Back in my room, I was certain that I would not be able to sleep. I flipped on the TV in time to see a friend of mine being featured on HBO's *Real Sex*. I had known her primarily as a playwright, and a damn good one. Her last play actually brought a tear to my eye, which never happens because I am almost entirely dead inside. I didn't know she also did sex work. You learn all kinds of things about people you know from cable TV sometimes. I'm glad I don't have HBO at home (also, I can't afford it). Turned it off and wrote some goofy gibberish I thought might work okay as a song.

And when I grow too old to dream / I'll climb inside a hole and sleep / and when I rise again, it'll be as something low /

something slow / at the left hand of Lucifer

The melody had been bouncing around in my head for a few days before that. I think it was based, loosely, on something some old crooner used to sing. *Sammy Davis Jr. maybe? Who's to say?* I even got a riff in my head for the melody line that fit pretty well. Too bad I don't write music anymore. I no longer even own a guitar, as I had hawked the last one for rent money. Oh well. I wrote down the melody and chord progression in my notebook anyway. Who knows, maybe I will use it again some sunny day.

From out of nowhere, another line popped into my head:

I feed pages through a crack in the glass.

"The fuck?" I said out loud to my spiral notebook as it lay spread open on the hotel room bedcover. I looked at the words again and again, but could not place them in any specific context.

I feed pages through a crack in the glass.

I could not fathom what it might possibly mean. Language devoid of context is simply noise. Meaningless barks and squiggles. *Should I build something around this line?* What would that be? Why did I even write it?

I receive pages through a crack in the glass, I wrote below it.

"That does not help," I said aloud to no one. I closed my notebook and tossed it to the floor.

I heard the text alert on my phone go *wmp wmp wmp.* Checked the screen. It was *her.*

> *R U still in town?*—she asked.
> *No*—I lied.—*Already in West Virginia*—
> *Y R U in WV?!*—She asked.
> *Ghost gig*—I said.
> *Is this going 2 be like that time U got brought in to do punch up for that movie script but when U arrived on set in that swamp in Missouri they had forgotten U were coming and did not need U anymore?*—

Does Missouri have swamps? I wondered. *I shall have to look that up.* (I didn't.)

*It was Mississippi—*I replied.—*And yeah, probably.—*

At least I got to hang out with a couple of Academy-Award-winning actors, I thought to myself. *And meet a bunch of cool blues musicians.* Too bad I fucking hate blues music.

*Fun times—*she said.

How's your pilot working out?—

It's working out.—

That's good.—

Miss U—

Do you actually?—

Yeah I think so. Maybe. Kinda.—

I miss you too. Goodnight.—

I turned off the phone and flipped the TV back on. My playwright friend was still going at it on HBO, now with another lady and a bald guy with a sculpted goatee. Flipped it off again. It was only 2am, but I knew I should probably try to snag some winks since I had to fly out before too long, and I was still a solid five-hour drive from LAX. Thankfully, I was a little high. That does help. I closed my eyes, and in the words of Jonathan Harker, "I did not sleep well, though my bed was comfortable enough, for I had all sorts of queer dreams."

When we arrived at the cabin, I stepped out of the car and breathed in the crisp country air. Even in the pitch of midnight I could see the wooded splendor of our surroundings: rolling acres of green, a tree-lined horizon, the moonlight cast like a shimmering white highway across the still water of the lake. Given the life I had lived of late, the life to which I had grown grimly and grimily accustomed, I could scarce believe that this would be my situation, if even only for a few days.

I grabbed my duffle and my book bag out of the back seat of my car.

"I brought some schoolwork with me," I said to Seth in a

hush. Not that there was anyone around to disturb, just the stillness itself. "If I get some done; great. If not, that's cool too."

"Take all the time you need," Seth replied, equally as quiet. He still seemed tense. The hour and a half drive had clearly not calmed his nerves. "In fact, it would probably be best to ease Emily into this. Don't push her. When she's ready to talk, she will. Until then, my house is your house. The fridge is packed, the bar is stocked. You are welcome to stay as long as you like...but...if at any time you feel the need to leave, just do it. Just do it. You have no obligation as far as I'm concerned."

"At least until we have contracts," I said. "I'll call Sal tomorrow."

"Okay, that's fine. I will stay tonight, but I need to head back to Wheeling first thing in the morning. I don't usually come back during the week unless I really have to, but if you need to call me, do so. And...if...if you need to call the police, don't hesitate." "Um...all right."

"I'll show you where the panic buttons are," he continued. "Do not be afraid to use them." Although I didn't say anything, I did find it more than a bit odd that Seth was willing to let a strange man stay at his remote house on the lake with his sister, alone and unchaperoned, for days on end. However, he seemed more concerned *for* me than *about* me. I was not quite sure how to feel about that, but it did put my teeth on edge just a bit. "You ready?" he asked. "Let's head in."

"I can't wait."

He put one boot on the bottom step, then paused. He turned to me and said, "It gets bad here at night sometimes."

"Okay."

Inside the cabin was warm and comfortable. For a young, single, straight(?) man, Seth Conlin had a good sense for decorating a rustic-yet-stylish log home. Or he had the good sense to hire someone who did. 2,500 square feet, natural, exposed woodwork, high ceilings, finished loft with private rooms, two bed, two bath, full kitchen, wrap-around porch that overlooks the lake, indoor and outdoor stone fireplaces. *I could live here. I could live here for a while.*

"There is an extra room upstairs," Seth whispered, "but if Em—"

"Couch is fine," I whispered in return.

We stood statue-still for a moment in perfect silence. Not a peep. After a good couple of seconds, Seth's face finally began to relax.

"I think," he whispered, "maybe, possibly, we just might—"

Suddenly, we heard a piercing wail from upstairs.

"NOOOOOOOOOOOOOOOOOOOOOO!   GET AWAAAAAAAYYY!"

"Fuck," Seth groaned, and ran upstairs. I heard the rattling of a doorknob. "Em! It's me! Open the door!"

"They're trying to get in!!!" I heard a woman shriek. "They know we're in here alone!"

"*I'm* trying to get in, Em!" Seth said, exasperated. "Move the bureau away from the door!"

"They're twisting the doorknob!"

"That's ME, goddamn it!"

"Seth?! the woman's voice cried.

"Yeah, Em, it's Seth. It's Seth. Let me in now."

I heard furniture scraping across hardwood floor and a door fly open. I couldn't see what was happening up there, but I heard muffled sobbing.

"Seth…Seth…I w-was so scared…"

"I know. I'm sorry I wasn't here. But I gotcha. I gotcha. Come on now."

I heard the door shut, and then *mostly* silence again.

Well, that was fun.

I plopped down onto the sofa and sank in, cashed out, welcoming another round of queer nightmares.

* * *

It was still dark when I felt myself being nudged awake.

"Hey," Seth whispered. "I need to head out."

"Sure, no problem," I said, sitting up. "Everything okay?"

"Oh yeah, she settled right down as soon as she got her head clear. Zonked out in minutes flat. She'll likely sleep into the day. But she will be up, eventually." Pause. "She'll be fine."

"Til the sun goes down?" I asked.

Seth proceeded to show me where the panic buttons were and assured me that the local PD knew the fastest route to the cabin. I guess I should have been concerned, but I really wasn't. The benefit of being dead inside, I suppose.

"Worry not, Mr. Conlin," I said. "All will be well."

"Okay, okay. I think so too. I think this will be good. For everybody."

"Agreed."

He smiled, looking at least somewhat relieved. I really liked his smile. "When you talk to Mr. Willis today, have him send me the contract in Wheeling. I will have my lawyer give a quick once-over, and then I'll get the money right to him."

"Sounds good. And don't worry about Emily. We'll be doing this dance at her tempo. No rush, no pressure. You have my solemn promise on that. And we'll make a good book. I promise that too."

"I appreciate ya, sir," he said. We shook hands, and he departed.

The cabin was still.

It was the most actual silence I had heard in quite some time. The low-level buzz that lives in my eardrums, but is usually muffled by the general noise of life, once again made its presence known. Through the window, I saw the top edge of the morning sun just beginning to peek up from behind the trees. I opened my bookbag, cut a modest rail on the back of one of my textbooks, and slammed it up my nose. I grabbed a tall can of Guinness from the bar mini fridge, then headed outside to greet the dawn.

The frosted dew on the grass crunched under my boots as I headed toward the lake. I popped the tab on the Guinness and let it breathe for a moment before taking a swig. It was good, though it mixed a bit with the taste of the coke. *Breakfast of champions.* Fog rolled up the hill over the short, stone retaining wall as the sun tossed a sheet of blood orange across the rippling water. I again took a deep breath of country air, but coughed a bit this time as invisible stalactites dripped chemical glaze down the back of my throat. I took another belt of Guinness.

Sitting on the wall, I pulled a pen and notebook out of my bookbag. I had been making an honest attempt to keep my professional writing notebooks and my school writing notebooks separate, but I was pretty sure they would all start to bleed together before too long.

On November 19th of 1957, four actors from the San Francisco Actors' Workshop performed Samuel Beckett's troubling, and troublesome, absurdist play *Waiting for Godot* for 1,400 of some of the nation's most dangerous inmates at San Quentin penitentiary. There had not been a performance of any sort at that prison since Sarah Bernhardt played a rare Christmas show there in 1913. *Godot* already had a problematic reputation, causing, as Martin Esslin claimed, "near riots among a good many highly sophisticated audiences in Western Europe" (*The Theatre of the Absurd* 1). But this play, with its meandering conversations, barren landscape, jokes about suicide, and most of all, the heart-breaking hopelessness of the protagonists desperately waiting for a visitor who is never going to come, spoke to these convicts in a very personal way. And where many non-incarcerated audiences saw deliberate obscurity and tedium for tedium's sake, the inmates saw within *Godot* unvarnished truth about the human condition as they understood it. "Godot is society," one prisoner told a reporter from the *San Francisco Chronicle* who was present. "He's the outside," the prisoner continued, and "...if Godot finally came, he would only be a disappointment" (Esslin 2). The inmates' emotional connection to this absurdist play makes intuitive sense, as day-to-day life within prison walls is innately absurd: every movement and activity is rigidly plotted, every day is constructed to be just like the day prior (and the next), and loneliness is yoked to a complete loss of privacy. And yet, even within the mundanity of unbreakable routine the threat of chaotic violence hangs ever-present.

Hmmm...decent, I thought. *Could use some work.* I had about two hundred pages of notes, odds and sods, bits and pieces of research, observation, and just general stuff crammed into various folders and binders. I kept hoping it would all make sense at some point, that the disconnected parts would come together on their own. Order and discipline have never been my strong suits. *Perhaps more booze would help. Perhaps I should just stare at the lake for a while.*

Feeling eyes upon me, I turned around. The space between the house and the lake was actually a bit greater than I had realized. Standing on the back porch of the cabin was the figure of a woman in gray. She waved her hand over her head; I waved back. She retreated inside. *Contextual analysis will have to wait, I suppose.*

* * *

I entered the cabin to the sound of Nat King Cole and the aroma of cooking eggs.

"Helloooo!" I heard a bright, sing-songy voice float from the kitchen. It was the same voice from last night, but much more cheerful.

"Emily Conlin?"

From around the corner came a woman in her early-to-mid thirties, if I were guessing, wearing an oversized gray crew-neck sweater and, perhaps, nothing else at all. I quickly realized that she was also wearing short shorts the exact same color as the sweater. She also wore what appeared to be a cherry-red anklet made from small, plastic beads, a fashion choice one might consider better suited to a girl in junior high rather than an adult woman, *but what do I know.*

"Yes! Hi! Yes, that's me! How are you?" She walked over to me, and we shook hands. "Would you like some tea?"

"Please."

She flittered back to the kitchen area. I followed her, leaning against the support beam that divided the main living room and the kitchen space. She dropped two tea bags into small ceramic cups of steaming water and flipped the eggs.

"Hungry?" she asked.

"Sure," I said, tossing the empty Guinness can into the recycling bin.

"I am soooooo sorry about last night," she said, grabbing a small carton of half-and-half from the refrigerator. "Do you want cream for your tea?"

"Not necessary."

"It is *so* embarrassing. I just get really disoriented these days when I wake up in the middle of the night by myself." Pause. "No, that's not right. I WASN'T by my *self*, that was the problem. I was not by my self because I *was* alone. I'm still not used to that. I get all turned around when I'm alone."

Um...okay...

"It's fine, Ms. Conlin."

"Gaaah, that sounds weird. Let's just go with Emily, 'kay?"

"Very well, Emily."

"But you're here now!"

"I'm sorry?"

"You're here now, so I'm not alone."

"Oh. Yes. That's true."

Emily scooped the eggs onto two plates, squeezed out the tea bags on a metal spoon, and tossed them in the trash. She danced a bit from counter to counter as she worked, humming along to the music. She was pretty, in a plain sort of way. Perhaps not as pretty as Seth was handsome, but comparable enough. You could certainly tell that they were siblings: same dark hair, though Seth's was tightly coiffed, and Emily's hung in tussled ringlets down to her shoulders. Same beautiful blue eyes, though Emily's were darker, more a midnight blue than sky. I could not really imagine her being a danger to anyone, *but then... with whose blood was she covered in the forest?*

"Should we eat outside? It's such a beautiful morning, yeah?"

One clear difference between her and Seth: the accent. Seth's was straight West Virginia. Hers, I could not place. It was mostly a flat, midwestern neutral, but there would occasionally be hints and flavors of other things. I could not pin it down.

"Sure," I said. "That would be nice."

I grabbed the plates, she grabbed the teas, and we headed out to the back deck.

"You're not cold?" I asked. The morning air was still crisp, and the breeze had a bite to it.

"Not at all," she replied. "In fact..." she stepped down off the deck into the grass. She spun around, soaking in the sun and cool air. "I wanted to walk out here before the dew frost melted and evaporated. I didn't feel grass on my feet for so long, now I want to every chance I get."

"Okay," I said. There was definitely something childlike about her. I wasn't yet sure if it was charming, or cause for alarm. *Perhaps both.*

"There!" she said with a big smile, kicking up her right leg. "Now my feet are nice and wet!"

"Rockin' good news."

She returned to the porch, sat down at the table with me, and we ate.

"The tea is okay?" she asked. "The eggs?"

"Delicious!"

"The secret ingredient is pepper."

"I won't tell anyone."

"Were you writing a school paper down there on the retaining wall?" she asked, her mouth half-filled with eggs.

"Yeah, I decided to go back. I have a degree in English already, but I felt like that probably wasn't enough, you know? So, we're trying a different angle."

"What's the new degree going to be about?"

"Humanities."

"Humanities? What's that?"

"I don't know. Made up shit."

"You don't have to make fun of me," she said. "It's not my fault I'm not educated." Pause. "Well, I guess it is partly my fault. But I'm trying to catch up. I do read a lot. Always have. I read some of your books. I like them!"

"Thank you. I'm not making fun of you. I really don't know how to explain the Humanities."

"Is it just the study of humans?"

"It's more like the study of the things that humans create."

"But isn't that, like, *everything* we learn in school?"

I had to stop and give that some thought. "Yeah... I suppose it is."

"I should probably go back to school too," she said. She took a sip of her tea and winced like it had burned her. She blew on it and took a lighter sip. I took a drink of mine. It didn't seem all that hot to me. "I thought that maybe I'm too old to go to school now, but you're older than me, I bet, yeah?"

"Maybe. But not by much, though. I look older than I really am. Let's just say the years have not been kind."

"Have the years not been kind, or have you just not been kind to yourself?"

"Myself doesn't deserve kindness," I said. "The prick bastard."

She stopped and stared at me, her eyes wide and round.

"Why would you say that?" she whispered.

Oh shit, I thought. *I hope I didn't trigger something.*

"Just a joke," I said. She continued to look at me askance, then returned to her eggs.

"Tell me more about Humanities," she said.

"Like I said, I'm not sure how to explain it. The focus of my study is mostly on how we use art to examine the nature of 'prison' in its myriad forms—both literal and figurative—as a social construct, and the invention of 'the self' within that construct. I am examining 'prison' and 'imprisonment' as social inventions and the role they play within the larger human experience. As we see in the writings of Michel Foucault and Erving Goffman, for instance, social systems of punishment and control—particularly, though not exclusively, the physical prison itself—have long utilized tropes and techniques that are highly and grotesquely theatrical, not to mention both *cruel* and *absurd*. There is an inherent artifice to human civilization itself, you know? Our languages, our clothing, our medicines, our governments, our philosophies and religions, all of our belief systems, our communities, are all constructs. Because of this, the entirety of the human experience can be seen as a palimpsest of artifice and fabrication, including the nature of the individual 'self.' *Prison*, then, whether physical or metaphorical, becomes a conceptual representation for *all* oppressive human constructs."

I finished my eggs. They were quite good.

"Huh," she said, sipping her tea. "I wouldn't know anything about that." I could have sworn she was being sarcastic, but I wasn't quite sure.

We sat, watching hawks fly over the water and occasionally swoop down to grab something out of the lake. Finally, I said, "So I have to ask; what's it like to be reunited with your brother again after all this time?"

"Okay, so, there is something you need to understand," she replied. "Seth was just a little thing when I disappeared. Like six or seven."

"Right?"

"But now...I mean, *he's all grown up now*. Has his own business and everything. Two houses! He was actually with me that day."

"He told me."

"He watched me walk up the steps to that creaky old porch and go inside..."

Uh...what's this now?

"Porch?"

"Yeah..."

"Okay?"

Don't rush her. Follow; don't lead.

"I've been having trouble sleeping lately," she said. "So instead of staring at the ceiling all night, I grabbed some books off Seth's bookshelf to read." *Déjà vu.* "First three were all yours, as serendipity would have it."

"Am I correct in assuming that my books have not aided your pursuit of a good night's sleep?"

We laughed.

"That would be a correct assumption, yes. No help at all in *that* department. But the more I read, the more I thought, *This is the writer I need to tell my story.*"

"I'm flattered."

"No, you're not. I know you're not, really. But that's okay."

"Admittedly," I said, "ghostwriting non-fiction is a special kind of hell for fiction writers. Real life seldom agrees to bend to your creative will."

We laughed.

"I get that," she said. "I do get it. I just think you're the rightest possible person for the job." Pause. "I noticed you write a lot about bloody stuff."

"Um...yeah, I suppose I do."

"A lot of blood. "

"Sure."

"Blood and screwing."

"Well...I mean...yeah, maybe. But...usually, you know, not at the same time."

"Just an observation."

"Thanks for noticing."

"I think it might probably be useful for our purposes."

The hell does that mean?

"Okay, well, that's why I'm here."

"And before we talk anything about money," she said, "I want you to know that I don't care about any of that stuff."

"Beg your pardon?"

"I mean, if we're talking about writing books and whatnot. Selling books. Selling the story for profit. You can keep all of it for all I care. Keep all the money, if there is any."

"Um..."

"I just need to get this out of my head." She tapped on her forehead.

"'*I am particularly oppressed,*'" I said, reciting, "'*by a certain memory from long ago. It came upon my mind vividly the other day, and ever since then it has stayed with me like an annoying tune. For some reason I think it will leave me alone once it is written down.*'"

"Who said that?"

"Dostoevsky. More or less."

"Oh, okay. Yep, that's where I'm at."

"Yeah…I hate to be the one to tell you, but it doesn't quite work that way."

"What do you mean?"

"Many people think of the writing process as *an exorcism* or something. But it's actually not. It's more like…draining a septic wound."

"That is…really gross."

"It is, yes."

Emily sat cross-legged on the chair, fidgeting with her plastic ankle bracelet.

"So, you talk like that all the time, yeah? That sounds like something one of your characters would say. But that's just you."

"So it would seem."

"You are definitely the best choice for this job."

"Well, I'm here. And my arsenal, such as it is, is at your disposal."

"Blood and screwing."

"Exactly. So…tell me about Down Pattersons."

"Okay…so…our town…it is a very, very, very small town."

"That is what I've heard."

"Quaint little place. Rustic. *Archaic.* Folks are friendly, if quiet. Coca Cola is 25 cents a can, cuz nobody ever bothered to update the machines. Things are fine and fair there in our little sleepy hamlet."

"Let's not get artsy just yet."

"Sorry. So, like, it's all good, and whatnot."

"Gotcha."

"But, like every nice little burgh that's worth a good goddamn…it's got its dark secret."

"Good," I said. "I like dark secrets."

She did not respond to that. We sat again in silence for a while, and I thought I might have derailed the thing again. But finally, she said, "Everyone always said the house was haunted, *so steer clear, now, hear?* But come on. When has 'the house is haunted' ever actually scared anybody away? Never, that's when."

Hmmmm...all right.

"Haunted, eh?"

"Yeah. But see...this house is different. People, when they talked at all about it, said it should be bulldozed. Claimed it's an eyesore. But that never happened. And it's not like it's out in the open or anything. It is nestled pretty far back in the woods. Nobody *ever* went in there. Nobody that I ever saw. We would hear stories of people who had gone in. Sometimes strangers in town on a dare, or something, from what we heard. They would roll into town to check it out. Then they would...vanish."

"And no one ever came asking after them?"

"Never. Occasionally, though—and it was rare, but it would happen—occasionally someone would *come out*. Sometimes screaming and jabbering. Sometimes...nearly mute. Sometimes d—...sometimes drenched in blood."

"Ah ha."

"But nothing ever came of it."

"What sort of nothing?"

"I mean like nothing. At all. They would be cleaned up, returned to their family if possible, or shipped away somewhere, never to be heard from again. There would never be an investigation. Or anything. The police would not ask questions."

"I took the liberty of contacting the Burlington PD," I said. "They informed me you had been catalogued as a missing person, but you were now found, and they were quite comfortable considering the matter closed. They had no knowledge of any other missing persons in the area and were otherwise not interested in speaking with me about it any further."

She turned her head to look at me.

"Can you see the surprise on my face?" she deadpanned. "This is me, doing my surprise face."

"It works. Very convincing."

"If we kids ever got too nosy," she continued, "we would be given just the barest of facts. 'That is Benny's uncle, Kurtis. We thought he had run off years ago, but I reckon he's been in that there house the whole time. He's all right now.'" She chuckled grimly and shook her head. "But...he was not all right. They were *never* all right. And nobody would ever say why. 'Just stay away from that house.' That's all they would ever tell us. 'Just stay away from it. Just stay away.' And everybody did. Just went about their days pretending the house wasn't back there, all tangled in among the brambles and briars." Pause. "*Nearly* everybody."

"But not you."

"I have always been a curious girl."

"What did the people say? The ones who had come out screaming. You said some were returned to their families. What did they say was in there?"

"Benjamin Haines, a boy two grades above me in school, his uncle had been in there. Everyone had figured him for dead. They had a funeral service and everything, I think. But one day he came out. One cold, blustery afternoon. Uncle Kurtis."

"Was he bloody?"

"He sure was."

"Was it his own blood?"

"That is a complicated question."

"No, it isn't."

"Only thing he ever said was...somebody asked him..." she proceeded to speak in two distinct voices, as if a pair of men were conversing. "'*Kurt*,' they said, '*Is the house haunted?*' and he answered, '*Yes.*' '*Haunted by what, Kurt?*' '*Me,*' he said."

"That's it?"

"That's it. *It is haunted by me.* Then one day he stuck a sawed-off under his chin and made his head a soup. Right there, all over his momma's kitchen."

"Jesus. And he was the only one to ever speak of it?"

"As far as I know."

"So... we may in fact be the first to ever go public with this?"

"It would seem."

I am ashamed of how delighted that little piece of information made me, but not nearly as ashamed as I should have been.

"What does the house look like?" I asked, regretting not having grabbed my notebook before we came out to the back deck (and forgetting the small spiral notebook I always keep in my jacket pocket). *Just listen now; get it on paper later.*

"Old," she said. "Of course. Rickety. Charred and smoky, where people had tried to burn it down and failed. The windows are busted out. On the outside. It looks empty and bare. From the outside. We never heard a sound from within. Not a peep. Not a creak. Which made the sudden random appearance of a screaming, flailing, occasionally blood-soaked person busting out the front door all the more peculiar."

"Yeah," I said, nodding my head. "That is not something you would want to get used to."

"You'd be amazed what you can get used to." Pause. "There was never any doubt in my mind that I would go in some day. It was never a question of if. Just a when. And six days after my fifteenth birthday seemed like as good a time as any. Seth and I were out walking in the woods, mushroom hunting as it were, and we just so happened to come across the house."

"Serendipitously enough."

"'*C'mon, Em, quit yer foolin' around,*'" Emily said, impersonating her seven-year-old brother. It was pretty spot-on. Nailed his lilt and cadence. "'*You stay away from that old place. I'm fixin' to tell Mama! Emily, come back*!!!'"

"And that was the last time you saw him? For twenty years?"

"No, not quite."

"Okay."

"Porch floorboards creaked under my feet. For one split second, I thought twice about opening the front door, and just turning tail and running. But…"

"You are a curious girl."

"Always have been."

"And so…"

"I stepped inside."

Emily Inside

"I take off my shoes by the door," Emily said. She stood up and pantomimed taking off a pair of shoes. She walked back into the cabin. I grabbed the dishes and followed her inside. "I respect the house," she continued. I could not quite tell what she was doing exactly, but if I were to wager a guess, she appeared to be recreating the layout of the place in her mind. I set the dishes in the sink and went to grab my notebook from the couch. "Living room..." she said. I wrote it down. "Parlor...Old, mauve, flower-print loveseat. Dusty coffee table. Full bookshelves, but nothing good. No blood and screwing. And the kitchen? Uncomfortably bright. Far too much natural light."

"What do you mean by that?" I asked.

"There is a skylight. A huge skylight. It's the only sun we have. We had. But...it is...concentrated. Even in the middle of the night, the moonlight would blast down through the glass in a solid beam. It was painful to the eye. And disorienting."

"I gotcha."

"Something funny, though. All the windows? Unbroken."

"The windows are broken outside the house, but unbroken inside?"

"I swear that it's true." Pause. "Dining room...Two, actually. Two full dining rooms, one upstairs and one downstairs. Identical in every way."

"Hold on a second," I said, trying to get down at least most of what she was saying. She paced about the main room of the cabin, only slightly aware of my presence just then. "We are not upstairs yet."

"Sorry," she said, absently. "Right. Downstairs. In the kitchen there were biscuits and marmalade sitting out on a tea tray on the marble counter. I took a bite of biscuit."

"Was it good?"

"It was okay. Kind of yeasty. I walked out to the living room. Wall-mounted mirrors in picture frames. No pictures, ever. Just mirrors. The dining room downstairs...both of them really...oak table, hand-stitched linens, seats exactly seven. Only odd numbers. Only ever odd numbers in the dining rooms. Somebody's idea of a joke. Rather cruel, really. Rather cruel."

"Only ever odd numbers..." I wrote that down. She appeared to consider it important information, so I thought it best to get it on paper.

"Suddenly," she said, turning quickly, "I saw two figures, barely visible, not much but shadows." Pause. "No...that's...that is not right. I saw one. One figure at first. A lady. Older, but not old. Fifty, maybe? She wore a white blouse and white dress slacks. Her hair was in a nice, sandy-blonde bob, and she had a nice face, and she was nice to me." Pause. "But...maybe a little...strained? I don't know how to say it."

"*Strained* works," I replied.

Emily said:

Strained. We'll go with that. Like, there was something insistent in her voice, but she was trying really hard to not sound like there was. "Hello there, young lady," *she said.* "I heard your feet creaking on the porch just now. I should tell you to leave immediately. But you wouldn't have come in if that sort of advice mattered to you."

"Who are you?" I asked.

"It's doesn't matter anymore," she replied.

"What's your name?"

"It doesn't matter anymore."

"My name is Emily Conlin."

"It doesn't matter anymore."

"It matters to me."

"Do you know yourself, then?"

"I should hope so."

"Wonderful. I wish nothing but the best for your sweet girl."

"My sweet girl?"

"For you. Sweet girl."

In the doorway to the kitchen, I saw someone else standing. Another woman, about the same build as the woman in white. But her face was covered, like by an old-timey wedding veil or something. I couldn't see her...I could not see her face at all. She retreated into the kitchen.

"Why is her face covered?" I asked.

"Oh, honey pie," the woman said, "you're not ready to meet her just yet."

"I'm curious about this house."

"Of course you are. Have a poke around. Some folks will be about later. You can say 'hello' and 'how do' if you've got a mind to. Later. Fruit cellar downstairs. All fresh pickings. Just be sure to avoid the cold storage deep in the back."

"How come?"

She was silent for a few moments. Then she said, "Sour meat, my dear. You don't want a taste of that." The woman with the veil appeared again. She put out her hand. The woman in the white blouse walked toward her, her hand outstretched. "The circle room waits for you upstairs, I'm sure," she continued. "But not until you are ready. There is tea in the fridge. Someone has fixed a fresh batch of biscuits and marmalade."

"Who did? Who prepared them?"

"It doesn't matter anymore." The woman in white and the shrouded woman retreated into the shadows, hand in hand. "Just to let you know," she said, "should you decide to stay, there will be screaming."

"Who were those women, Emily?" I asked.

Emily turned to look at me, nearly startled, as if she had

forgotten I was there. I indicated that there was room on the couch. She declined.

"They were my friends," Emily said, small but direct.

"I sincerely doubt that."

"They were."

"In what way were they your friends?"

"In what way is anybody friends with anybody?"

Okay.

"And how about the cellar. Did you check it out?"

"Yes… eventually…"

"Was it cold?"

"It was so… so cold…"

I should have noticed her trembling. But I didn't. I guess I chose not to notice.

"And the storage room?"

"Ohhhh…" she whimpered, flapping her hands at her side.

"Tell us about the cold storage, Emily."

She collapsed at the waist and screamed—a wrenching, piercing scream.

"AAAAAAAAAAAAAAAAAAAAAAAAAAAAAAAAAAAAA!!!!!"

Shit.

"Emily?"

She banged herself on the head with her fist and pulled her own hair.

"NOOOOOOOOOOOOOOOOOOOOOOOOOOOOOOOOOOOOOOO!!!!"

I leapt off the couch and grabbed her. I knew I had no right to put my hands on her, and I probably should not have, but I panicked. I just didn't know what else to do. I untangled her hair from the fingers of her right hand and held both of her wrists tight to stop her from hurting herself. I thought I might need to make my way to the nearest panic button by the hall closet, but for the moment, I just held her as she thrashed and wailed.

Eventually, she fell into me, sobbing.

"I'm sorryyyyyyyyyy..."

"It's okay, shhhhh shhhhh," I said. "It's okay..."

"I'm sorry," she cried. "I'm s-s-s-s-sorry...I'm sorry..."

"We don't need to do this now."

"I'm so -*sob*- sorry..."

I was pretty sure that she was not actually speaking to me. This was an apology to someone who was not present.

"It can wait," I said. "It can wait. We can talk about it later."

"Yeah... okay... yeah... later... later..."

I led her over to the couch. I continued to hold her as she cried. It was a very uncomfortable situation. *I am not trained for this.*

After a while, she calmed down.

"Are you all right?" I asked.

She sat up, wiping her eyes on the backs of her hands and the long sleeves of her gray sweater. "There will be screaming," she sniffled. I chuckled. She chuckled.

"Fair enough."

"I would... really like a glass of wine," she said with a sigh. "Would you like to have a bit of wine with me?"

"Well..." I said, "I'm not really much of a drinker." She laughed with a snort, which made us both laugh. "But sure. I shall crack a bottle at once."

I popped the cork on a bottle of *Chateau le Thys*. She ordered some Chinese food for dinner. The closest place was in Grafton, apparently, and the local police had not shared their shortcut to the cabin. Emily said it would be sundown by the time the food was delivered. So, we had a few glasses as we walked around the grounds and talked about anything other than the house on the outskirts of Down Pattersons.

* * *

"Do you like poetry?" she asked. The wind at midday had not warmed much, but even still it seemed she was not cold.

"I do, yes," I replied. "I don't write a lot of it these days, because I don't really write music anymore."

"What does that have to do with anything?"

"I just...they're connected. In my mind, they're connected."

"Okay."

"But I do still like to read it. I am a bit of a boring snob, though, cuz I only actually like poetry from dead people."

"Well, that is just a crying shame," she said. "We should celebrate the living while they're still living, no? Death comes soon for everybody, after all, and it comes in heaps and piles."

"That is a...very odd way to put that," I said (making a mental note to write it down later). "But I get what you're saying. And you're right."

"What is the best poem of all time, in your opinion?" she asked. "What is your all-time favorite?"

"That is two separate questions," I replied. "My favorite poem is 'The Bells' by Edgar Allan Poe. Just to read it will cause a cacophonous racket inside your skull that will drive you insane. I love that."

"But it's not the best?"

"No, the greatest poem in the English language is 'Dream Variations.'"

"By Langston Hughes," she said. "I remember reading that in tenth grade English. Last English class I ever took. Forgive me if my memory is wrong, but isn't that just the same stanza repeated?"

"It is," I said. "But with ever-so-slight word changes which alter the entire meaning of the piece. Many have tried to replicate it, but Hughes has no equal. He stands alone."

"I should reread that," she said. She downed the rest of her wine with a shudder. "My favorite poem is a lot newer. In fact, I just read it for the first time recently. Like your work, and everything else these days, I found it in a book on my brother's shelf."

"What is it?" I asked.

"It goes:
Poetry was popular in Hell, the shades
Recited lines they had memorized—forgetful
Even of who they were, but famished for life."

"Ah yes, Robert Pinsky!" I said. "'Eurydice and Stalin,' that is a great one. Okay, I take it back, there are a handful of great poets who are still alive. I talked to Pinsky on the phone last year, serendipitously enough. Really nice guy, helluva writer."

"Why did you talk to him on the phone?"

"I wanted to send him a copy of my latest book. Latest at the time. He said that was fine, that he looked forward to reading it, so I printed it out and mailed it to him. Drained two ink cartridges, filled three shoeboxes. I should have just had my agent send him a copy, but I have been known to be impulsive on occasion."

"No kidding," she deadpanned.

"I mean…poet laureate, you know?"

"*Laureate?*" she echoed. "What a weird sounding thing."

"Yep."

"What does it mean?"

"Um…" Pause. "Why is 'Eurydice and Stalin' your favorite poem?"

"Because it speaks to me," she said, walking toward the lake. "It *is* me."

I stopped to ponder what she could mean by that. *Nope…I got nothing.*

"'*Shame, endless revision, inexhaustible art,*'" I recited, following her down.

"'*She crossed the bridge and wandered across a field of steaming ashes,*'" she replied without turning around.

Emily walked around the retaining wall to the bottom of the hill. There at the lake was a small, wooden boat dock.

"Does Seth have a boat?" I asked.

"I don't actually know," she said. "I don't really come down here much. Never learned to swim." She stepped cautiously toward the water's edge, looked down, then immediately backed away.

"Did you see something?"

"Let's go back," she said quickly.

"How come?"

"I'm just not ready yet."

"Ready for what?"

"I mean… I want to lie down a bit before the food arrives. You could maybe get some schoolwork done, yeah? Then you can tell me all about it over dinner. Since I have so much to learn. And we can finish the wine too."

"Okay, sure. If that's what you want to do."

She started back up the hill. I walked down to the dock. The water was still, but for the insects gliding across the surface.

"That's dangerous," she shouted down to me. "That's dangerous down there."

"I can swim," I said.

"I'm barefoot at least," she said. "Those heavy boots you wear will drag you all the way down."

"Nah."

I turned to follow her back up the hill, past the wall.

"Be careful you don't overestimate yourself," she said over her shoulder.

"That is what I do," I replied.

She chuckled, dryly. "I'll bet."

"So tell me, Emily, did Pinsky get it right?"

"Get what right?"

"Is poetry popular in Hell?"

She stopped halfway up the hill and turned to face me, panting slightly, her brow furrowed, beaded with sweat despite the cool breeze. "What a mean thing to ask me."

"I am kind of a mean person."

"I don't believe that" she said. She turned back around and continued walking. "I think you are actually very kind. And I'm a good judge of character."

"Are you though?"

45

"I would like to think so."

"You've seen what I do to my characters."

"I have," she replied. "You've certainly created and then crushed your share of them." *True enough,* I thought. *And I don't do sequels. Use once and destroy.* Then she said, "I have too."

We walked the rest of the way to the cabin in silence.

Back inside, Emily told me that the food was already paid for, I just needed to give the delivery guy a tip. I figured it should be a pretty generous tip, given the drive the poor fellow would have to make, and she agreed. She headed up to her room for a nap, then stopped toward the top of the stairs.

"You know," she said, "there are two bedrooms up here. You don't have to stay on the couch."

"I wouldn't presume to climb into Seth's bed without a direct invitation," I replied. "Maybe someday."

"I can never tell when you're joking."

"Neither can I."

"Wake me up when dinner is here," she said. And with that, she retired.

Within his seminal work *Discipline and Punish (1975)*, Michel Foucault explores how modern modes of discipline and punishment, with their principles of order and control, tend to "disindividualize" power, making it seem as if power is simply inherent within the prison, the school, the factory, as opposed to being a deliberate construct. The Panopticon, with its all-seeing authoritarian eye, becomes Foucault's model for the way other institutions function. "Power has its principle not so much in a person as in a certain concerted distribution of bodies, surfaces, lights, gazes; in an arrangement whose internal mechanisms produce the relation in which individuals are caught up" (202).

I poured myself a short glass of wine and corked the bottle. I did have a lot of schoolwork to do, but I wasn't quite sure what was most pressing at that moment. It remained a lot of angles without a clear, singular vision. And deadlines have never been my friends.

In discussing the history and evolution of punishment in the Western world from the 18th Century on, Foucault discusses the "theater of punishment" prior to the mainstreaming of the prison concept and the necessity of the "audience" for public torture, execution and mockery of the convicted. I see Foucault's considerations of the complicity of the crowd/audience in the degradation of accused criminals explained rather clearly by Erving Goffman in his first and greatest work, *The Presentation of Self in Everyday Life*. Here, Goffman asserts that we are already predisposed toward "acting" in the public environment, adopting roles to play, even creating "sets" upon which to perform. As such, just as actors look to their director and dramaturge for guidance on how to behave and present themselves, so too are individuals within the society inclined to follow the direction of the power system, regardless of what those directions may be. "In their capacity as performers," Goffman claims, "individuals will be concerned with maintaining the impression that they are living up to the many standards by which they and their products are judged" (162). These performances exist primarily to avoid embarrassment, confusion and confrontation, not for moral reasons. Instead, as performers, Goffman continues, "individuals are concerned not with the moral issue of realizing these standards, but with the amoral issue of engineering a convincing impression that these standards are being realized. Our activity, then, is largely concerned with moral matters, but as performers, we do not have a moral concern in these moral matters. As performers we are merchants of morality" (162). And even as spectators, we are still performers. Foucault presents this dynamic in his examination of the 18th Century practices of public torture and execution; what he called "the spectacle of the scaffold."

I popped a handful of vikes and washed it down with the *Chateau le Thys* because I am classy.

Instant regret.

My skin got hot, and my stomach churned. I ran to the bathroom to puke. I retched a few of the pills back up, but not all of them. *What a waste.*

"The public execution then has a juridico-political function" Foucault explains. "Its aim is not so much to re-establish a balance, as to bring into play the dissymmetry between the subject who has dared to violate the law and the all-powerful sovereign who displays his strength" (48-49). The public spectacle of violence toward the prisoner is a "liturgy of punishment," an "affirmation of power and of its intrinsic superiority" that must "display its pomp in public" wherein the accused is not just beaten and broken but humiliated, while the sovereign is flanked on all-sides by guards and soldiers (49). The imbalance of power is so severe it is nearly ludicrous: a burlesque of justice.

I stood up to splash some water on my face and noticed that there was no mirror over the bathroom sink. Where a mirror would typically be was a framed painting of a Florida panther with a rattlesnake draped across its shoulders. *Or is it a leopard?* I would come to discover that there was not a single mirror in the entire cabin. *Why would there be no mirrors? Maybe Seth just isn't a vain guy. Yeah...right. That dude's haircut cost more than my rent.*

> Foucault illustrates instances of the public's sympathy shifting toward, and in favor of, the condemned and their rage turning toward the executioners (and even the sovereigns). These instances, though relatively few in number, were sufficient to cause a reconsideration of how state-enforced punishments were to be carried out. In these rare but notable instances prisoners—usually those accused of "rioting," or house servants and lower-caste workers whose infractions seemed minor to the larger population—were freed (and even cared for) by the mob, gallows were obliterated, executioners were killed. (Foucault gives the example of a riot in Paris in 1761 in support of a servant girl who had stolen a bit of cloth from her master. "Despite the fact that the woman admitted her guilt, handed back the material and begged for mercy, the master refused to withdraw his complaint; on the day of the execution, the local people prevented the hanging, invaded the merchant's shop and looted it; in the end, the servant was pardoned," and

even a woman who attempted to stab the master with a sewing needle was only banished for three years [62]). Clearly, the power structure demanded a less messy, more orderly, more absolute, more omniscient, and more coldly impersonal (yet supposedly more civilized and humane) system of punishment. And so, the prison as we know it was born, and with it the Panopticon of the surveillance state we have come to know and accept today…

There was a knock at the front door of the cabin. I wiped my lips across my sleeve and walked out to answer it. As I opened the front door, I noticed that it had gotten dark out already.

"My man," I said to the friendly young cat shivering on the porch.

"Good evening, Mr. Conlin," he said to me, handing over the bags of food.

"Um—"

"The extra egg rolls are in the smaller bag. Your wife was HELLA-insistent that we were not to bring any fortune cookies. Like, big-time insistent."

"Yeah, she is awfully superstitious, that wife of mine."

"So, I am pretty sure that there aren't any in there, but—"

"Not to worry, my friend," I said. "If I see any, I'll shove them in my pocket straight away. She will be none the wiser. I could use some extra fortune, anyway."

I gave him a $20 tip which he seemed quite pleased about, and he went upon his way.

"Em!" I shouted up the steps. "Dinner!"

"Okay," I heard her reply, then I heard the sound of the bureau scraping across the hardwood floor. *Can never be too safe, I guess.*

* * *

Emily came down the steps wearing a dark red crew neck sweater exactly like the one she had worn earlier, but for the color. Her hair had been brushed, but it was still quite tussled. She had also changed her ankle bracelet. This one was equally cheap looking and plastic, but rainbow-colored. As she got closer, I noticed she had applied some mascara and a bit of eyeliner as well, which had to have been tricky with no mirror.

"Good news," I said, "they threw in some extra fortune cookies."

"What?!" She scrunched up her face in a scowl. It was kind of adorable. "I told them specifically... You're teasing me, aren't you."

I shrugged. "Who's to say?"

"You are just the worst person ever," she said, and walked over to the iPod on the table. She tapped it on, and Billie Holiday began to sing through all the speakers in the cabin.

"Totally."

"Eat on the deck?" she asked.

"Okay, but I'm going to put a fire on."

"That sounds amazing."

We retreated to the back porch. She spread the food out on the table and poured the wine. I put logs in the fireplace. Oak and pine, nice and dry. They caught quickly in a beautiful orange flame. It was a particularly chilly evening. Emily put on neither shoes nor long pants, but she did toss a white wool scarf around her neck. I zipped my jacket up all the way. I was still cold.

"I've been thinking some more about your buddy Pinsky's poem," she said, going straight for the eggrolls. "Eurydice is a figure from mythology, right?"

"That is correct."

"So why take a mythic character out of her context? Ancient times were...well, ancient times. Right? Life is different now. Way different."

"Myths offer a sort of conceptual shorthand," I said, digging into my *er kuai* spicy chicken, "presenting recognizable archetypes in both character and circumstance that are familiar to the audience, even if the specific stories are not intimately known to each and every individual audience member. Their elements are ephemeral within the culture. The myth of Narcissus and Echo, for instance, is one whose names and concepts are ingrained in Western culture even for those who might not be able to recall the finer details of the story."

"Do I know that one?" she asked, more to herself than to me. "I don't think I know that one."

"Sure you do. It's imprinted in your DNA."

"Hmm."

"Within the classic narrative," I said, topping off both of our wineglasses, "the 'talkative' mountain nymph Echo is cursed by the goddess Hera after Hera wrongly assumes the girl had deliberately distracted her."

"Distracted her from what?"

"From catching her husband Zeus in the act of fucking the ever-loving hell out of a group of other nymphs."

"Oh. Of course."

"According to Hera's curse, Echo is doomed to only repeat back what has been said to her, forever lacking words of her own. Shortly thereafter, Echo sees and falls in love with the beautiful but arrogant hunter Narcissus who spurns everyone's love, man and woman alike. Unable to communicate with Narcissus except to parrot his every word, which enrages him, Echo runs off heartbroken, and dies, leaving only her cursed echo to reverberate through the valley. Hera feels guilty for Echo's demise, and curses Narcissus too. Narcissus then falls in love with the only face worthy of his beauty: his own reflection in the river. Unable to touch the object of his affection, he wastes away...or commits suicide...frozen by longing for himself."

"Good god," Emily said, noticeably disturbed. "I hate that story."

"I know, it is really sad. I always wish I could rescue poor Echo."

"Narcissus too, really. Why did Hera curse him?"

"She was quite the spiteful one."

"All because Zeus was fucking a bunch of girls. Typical."

"Well...nymphs."

"So, like, *little girls?*"

"An important thing to remember," I said, "is that Zeus, like every single god ever, is a despicable sack of shit."

We talked the night away, polishing off a bottle. Then another. After a while we simply sat in silence, settled deeply into the outdoor sofa, the fire crackling, Billie Holiday crooning on the stereo, watching the tree branches dance in the breeze. Emily put her knees under her chin, stretched her oversized sweater over her bare legs, and drifted off to sleep. I hadn't felt particularly tired, but I must have drifted off as well.

When I opened my eyes, I was alone on the sofa. Within the stone fireplace were glowing red coals, but no flame. The wind was in-your-bones cold. I walked over and peeked my head inside the door to the cabin.

"Em?"

No answer.

I went upstairs. Both bedrooms were empty, as was the upstairs bathroom. The wall was naked above the bathroom sink, where a mirrored cabinet had clearly once been. My throat went dry, and the hairs stood up on the back of my neck. "Emily?" I shouted louder as I ran down the stairs. Nothing.

I ran back to the deck and jumped down into the grass. *Where the fuck is she?!* I didn't want to yell into the night. I didn't know what time it was, but it had to be late. I wasn't sure where the nearest neighbors were either, but regardless, I did not want to cause a scene.

As I started down the hill toward the lake, I spotted her white wool scarf muddy on the ground.

Fuck...what the hell...

I could hear faint singing. I walked faster, careful not to trip and tumble on the uneven ground.

As I got to the retaining wall, I could tell that it was Emily. My eyes adjusted to the dark and I could vaguely see her down below, sitting cross-legged on the tiny boat dock, leaning over, peering directly into the still water.

"Emily, what are you doing?"

She did not respond, just continued singing. I headed down toward the dock. I could not tell what she was singing at first. The closer I got, the more I could make it out.

"Hold the moon my dear / Steal it clearly feeling healed / Leering through the clearing field / Nearly keeping sealed in fear..."

"Emily! Don't move, I'm coming down!"

"Old, the morning dear / Fear it, keep it sealed in steel / Praise it happening as often / Scream and scrape the lid of my coffin..."

I stepped onto the dock. She continued leaning over the edge, staring straight into her own reflection in the obsidian mirror of the lake.

"Em," I said gently, but firm, "could you, like, scooch back from the edge there, please? You are making me really nervous right now."

"Sometimes I think about following her," she said quietly, continuing to stare at her rippling reflection. "All the way down."

"I don't like that," I said. "I do not like that one bit."

"Isn't it crazy?" she said. "If I just dip my toes in, she will vanish."

"It is precisely talk like this that gets panic buttons pressed, Emily."

She turned around to face me. "I'm here alone most of the

time," she said. "If I was going to do it, don't you think I would have well before now?" Pause. "I haven't even taken you upstairs yet."

"That is true, you haven't."

"Do you have your notebook?"

I tapped my jacket pocket. "I have this one," I said. "I keep a small spiral notebook and pen in this pocket at all times."

She nodded. "Should we go upstairs, then? Now? To the circle room?"

"I can't wait."

"We always called it the circle room," Emily said. "But the room itself was not actually a circle at all. If anything, it was a perfect square. Total symmetry." She stood up, indicating the squareness of the boat dock. "The carpet was pure black. Baby-blanket soft under my bare feet." She swayed softly, gliding her bare soles against the splintery, untreated wood planks. "Against opposite walls to my left and to my right stood two identical red, crushed velvet divans."

"Identical?"

"In every way."

"Okay."

"And there, across the room, standing in the opposing doorway…there she was."

"Who was it?"

"It was her."

"It was who?"

"It was me."

"Who was who?"

"She was me."

"Emily Conlin?"

"But that doesn't matter anymore."

In the Circle Room

We choose a divan and sit. Of course, we choose the same one. We are, for the moment, indistinguishable. That one renegade hair in my left eyebrow, she has that. The polish on her toes is chipped like mine. Back when I still bothered to paint my toes. Every feeling, every freckle, every thought, every memory up until the moment our eyes first met, identical in every way. We are the same girl.

We are the same girl.

I don't know who said hello first. I don't know which one I was. I don't know which one I am. It doesn't matter anymore, I guess. She is...pretty. But not as pretty as I wish she was. We like to think we look as nice as our last, best photo. But she didn't. So, of course, we didn't. I read once, in a book from the bookshelf in the parlor, that there is a documented phenomenon, particularly amongst tribal people in developing areas of the world, who see their photograph for the first time, wherein they will deny themselves. Deny that it is actually them in the picture. "That is definitely not me; I'm not that old." "I'm not that skinny," and so on. That denial happens in the circle room. Sometimes fatally.

I felt like someone should speak, but...what could either of us say? We had nothing but the same information to share. The same thoughts. The same life experiences, limited though they were.

We sat and stared in the circle room. Stared into each other's dark blue eyes. For hours. In silence. It is common, though not universal. Face to face with yourself. Reactions vary. But finally, I was just about to say, "Let's leave," and she said, "Let's leave."

And in that brief moment, we were suddenly slightly different people. She was slightly faster. By the chaos of chance. How much are we shaped by chaos and chance? We are only shaped by chaos and chance. That's a good line. You should keep that.

The second-story corridor is a row of facing doors. Near perfect symmetry. We each took a side and tried them, knob after knob. We wondered, Were they locked? As we would come to discover, they were blocked. You could tell that someone had wedged something heavy against the other side.

We saw a man, slightly disheveled, standing at the very end of the hall. Twice our age, or nearly that. Staring at us intently. We backed up. He stomped toward us with stride and purpose. With his left fist, he knocked on one of the doors as he passed. Another man came out from that door, also disheveled, identical to him in every way but for their slightly different outfits. They walked toward us, the second man only slightly behind the first.

"You're new?" one of them said.

"What now?"

"Find a room, of course."

"We want to leave."

"The house?!"

"Yes!"

"TOGETHER?!"

"OF COURSE!"

"Have fun working that out!" He laughed. They both laughed.

"Why are you laughing? Why is that funny?"

"We've been here quite a while, girls. Quite a while. And you will be too. Might as well accept it."

"How long?"

"Long enough. You wanna fuck?"

"No, we don't."

"We'll make you come harder than you ever done did."

"No, we don't want you to."

"Then forget about him. Why don't you both come here and double-bob on this right here." He grabbed his crotch.

"NO! We don't want to!"

"You will before too long," he sneered. "Fuckin' drippy little cunts."

We ran down the stairs hand in hand, straight toward the front door. There was only one pair of shoes, but who needs them anyway. I have run through those woods in my bare feet plenty of times. Emily grabbed the handle and threw open the door.

"You can't both go, honey pies," said the woman in white, sipping tea on the flower-print loveseat.

"Why not?"

"Only one comes in, only one leaves."

"What?! Why?!"

"Oh, come now. How would your parents feel with two of the exact same daughter? That wouldn't do at all."

"What happens if we try?"

"First to have even just her toes cross the threshold is free to go about her business. The other will never make it out the door. Any door. Trapped. Forever."

"What?!"

"That's right, sweeties. That is how it is. So...which will it be? How will you choose? You could flip a coin, I suppose."

"We can't do that!"

"Well, why do you think we are all here? Because who could choose? And how? So long as you have each other, there is always the hope. If you find yourself alone, well...that is the end of hope, isn't it, sweet girls."

And Emily said, "But I've heard of people getting out! That lady from the library back when! And Benny's uncle Kurtis! How did they break free?"

"Yes. How indeed," the woman said with a nod. "How indeed. What did they have to do to themselves? To their selves. What would they have to do? How long before you can no longer trust your self?"

"Where is your other?" I asked.

"*She is sick right now. Just a bit of a headache.*"

"*But not you?*"

"*Not yet. We spend time apart. That is an option. But for now, I suggest you stock up on food from the kitchen. Things that will last. Then find a bedroom. And stay there. Until you are ready to venture out. Barricade the door. Open it for no one. No matter how hard they bang. No matter how or what they scream. Night is coming soon. It gets bad here at night sometimes. Try to ignore what you hear through the walls. You seem like such dear girls. I am sad for what you are bound to finally see here.*"

I finally coaxed her back up the hill to the deck. She refused to go inside the cabin. I think she was quite a bit drunker than I had realized. There was a quarter of a bottle of wine left, and I let her have the rest of it. I tossed some more logs on the smoldering fire and stoked it back to flame. Then I went inside and grabbed a down comforter from Seth's bed. I insisted she wrap herself in it as we sat again on the outside sofa.

"Daddy too too coldy so baby need-a bundle up," she simpered in a mocking, pouty, little-girl voice that made my skin crawl. But I would not be deterred.

"That is correct," I said, patiently waiting with notebook and pen in hand. *Follow; don't lead.*

I can't remember if there was still music playing or not. I never shut it off, but I do not recall anything but silence at that point, save the wind.

Finally, she said, "He was right."

"Beg your pardon?"

"He did make me come. Hard. They both did. They all did."

"Let's...unpack that a bit, shall we?"

Pause.

"No, I don't think so."

"Okay."

"The first night was rough," she said. "There was screaming all night. We found a small room of our own, with a window looking out into the woods. We barricaded the door with a chest of drawers. Just as we were told. Sat on the bed and watched the doorknob rattle and twist. They knew we were new. They knew we were soft. They wanted in. We pressed our feet against the dresser and hoped we were strong enough. We cried. We wanted Mommy to hold us and make it all better. We were sixty yards away from her. We would never see her again. She died six years ago. We were locked up inside."

"Did you talk, you and Emily?"

"We tried. But about what? How scared we were?"

"The window. You thought about it."

"No."

"Of course you did. You could have escaped right then and there."

"NO. I couldn't."

"Sprained an ankle, broken a leg, maybe, but you could have made it. You thought about it. You had to."

"No! I couldn't even think it, because then that would mean that she was probably thinking it too. So I willed myself not to think it."

"That's absurd. You can't will yourself to not think something. The act of willing it means you were thinking of it."

"This is *my* story!"

"And you're telling it wrong!" *Whoa! Check yourself, motherfucker!* "Look...you are not being honest with yourself. And if you're not honest with yourself, then you're not going to be honest with me. And then we can't do this thing."

"I was always honest with *my self*. And she was with me."

"I'm sure." Pause. "The first night was rough."

"The first night stretched on for days and nights. The days outside were bright and cheery, but we did not dare move the barricade. The nights were filled with screams, and bangs, and rattling doorknobs. Stir crazy and hungry and nothing to talk about but dull, old memories. But not really old enough to be old. You know? *Remember when... remember when...*"

"That lady told you to stock up on food."

"We were fifteen. We didn't listen."

"Of course."

"Came to find out later that we beat the odds simply by not tearing each other to pieces on sight."

"You mean literally?"

"I mean literally. Killing. Many people, otherwise decent, pleasant people, will meet themselves for the first time and lunge straight at each other. Teeth-to-throat. Faces hacked and torn to shreds."

"I like it."

"I don't know what that says about them."

"Nothing good, I would say."

"Then some are so captivated on sight they waste away, staring longingly into each other's eyes."

"It is the greatest love of all."

"You're mocking me."

"Not on purpose. Go on."

"Some are so captivated on sight they waste away, staring longingly into each other's eyes."

"But not you."

"It's like I said, she was pretty."

"Uh huh."

"She was very, very pretty." She indicated herself, wrapped in the down blanket. "See?"

"I do indeed."

"I was not disappointed."

"You don't have to convince me."

She took a long swig from the wine bottle.

"It wasn't until the fourth night barricaded in that room together that we made love." Pause. "Wouldn't you?"

Probably.

"Probably."

"I don't hear any judgment in your voice."

"There is none to hear. I've been to jail before." *Several times.*

"We made love to each other a lot. We made love all the

time, really. We were scared, and it felt good, and it passed the time and..."

"She already knew what you liked."

"She already knew."

"I get it."

"More than that, she knew all the dark things. The deep-down things. The things I never would have told a *real* lover. The things I never would have told anyone. Ever."

"Until now."

"I guess." Pause. "Do you have dark things deep down? Pshhh, that was a dumb question. I've read your books."

"They're obviously not too deep down if I put them in a book. Now here's *your* chance."

"Like draining a septic wound."

"Some would say."

She finished the rest of the wine, then set the bottle on the floor.

"We made love all the time," she said. "But I didn't *love* her...I didn't *fall in love* with her...until she finally stopped being me. Or...I stopped being her."

"How long did that take?"

"How long? What is time? Time is eternal."

"Eternity is a human construct," I said. "Therefore, it is finite." *That's a keeper!* I wrote that down both for the school-work *and* this book. "So, when she stopped being you, whom did she become?"

"Oh, many people," she replied winsomely. "Boyfriends, husbands, daughters, popes, movie stars, investment bankers, lion tamers, psycho killers, ranch hands, Can Can girls. And I did too. Never at the same time, of course. I was champion quarterback for quite a while."

"Congratulations."

"Emily loved that one."

"I have no doubt."

"We joined the others, eventually. We learned to deal with

the screaming at night. We learned to cope and survive. Over time, the house became... home. In time, you learn to take comfort in your confined space."

"So, when she stopped being you, that's when you fell in love with her."

"No," she said, a frustrated tone creeping in. "You misunderstand me. It was years later. And she wasn't her then. She wasn't me either. I fell in love with a man named Jason."

"He had a name?"

"It mattered. It still does. He was incredible. So much better than every other man in the house. He was the best a man could ever possibly be."

"Because you invented him."

"To my exact specifications. To ours."

"And what became of Jason?"

"She got tired of Jason. She wanted to be someone else instead of Jason. I protested. I wanted Jason. She didn't want to be Jason anymore. So she made Jason go away. I was angry. I wouldn't have done that to her. I was everybody she wanted me to be. Always. Without complaint. Without protest. So, I had to go elsewhere. Away from her. We spent time apart. We saw others. Eventually, we saw all the others."

"I sense that 'saw' is a euphemism here."

"It was entirely her fault."

"That seems unlikely."

"I'm kind. She is selfish."

"And yet... you're here. She's not."

"Yes..."

"Where is she, Emily? Where is Emily now?"

There was a long pause in the conversation. I did not prod her, although I must admit that I wanted to. But instead, I just waited. Patiently. Emily's look was inscrutable. She stared out at the lake. I suspected she longed to look at it more closely again. Then, she put her face in her hands and began to weep.

"We had lost all sense of time!" she cried. "Days and nights and years bled into one another. And they bled and bled. Always bleeding. Always...Is that -*sniff*- too artsy?"

"It's fine, Ms. Conlin."

"And then one day, on a day...a day like any other day...we awoke early for some reason. We were back together again, bored with making the rounds. Bored with everyone."

"Everyone who wasn't Emily."

"As we were dressing that morning, we looked out our window, two floors up, and we saw a young man stepping out of the woods. Seventeen, maybe. Eighteen. Maybe twenty. He stepped through a stand of Siberian larch out into the side yard near the bramble patch, wandered about, looking at the house, keeping his distance. *A new guest*, we thought. *That would be fun*. Hadn't been many fresh visitors in a while at that point. We started plotting our designs on him right away. And then suddenly Emily shouted, 'It's Seth!'"

"We ran downstairs to the parlor window, and there he was, staring straight in through the glass. He had grown so tall. 'Seth!' we screamed. 'Seth, it's Emily! Look at us! It's Emily! LOOK AT US!' We pounded on the glass. We tried to pry the window open. But we couldn't. It wouldn't budge no matter how hard we tried. We screamed and screamed...but he never heard. He never saw. We screamed, 'Don't go away! Don't leave us! DON'T LEAVE US!'"

"But..."

"But...after a bit, he just moseyed on. He was a man now. He had his own life. And so, he moved on. To make better choices than his big sister had."

"Have you spoken with him about that day?"

Pause.

"He's too embarrassed to say, you know, but he wants me to get your autograph. He was so excited you agreed to meet with me."

"Emily..."

"Yes. We talked about it. Some. We cried. He said he was

so, so sorry. He said he could not see me that day. There was nothing, he said, through the broken windows."

"*Couldn't see us*, you mean."

"That isn't what I said."

"What have you told him?"

"About what?"

"About any of it. About all of it."

"Close to nothing. He doesn't need details."

"He's going to know soon. If all goes as planned, you're telling the whole world here, you understand?"

"He won't read it. My curiosity is not his crime."

"Curiosity is not a crime."

"Maybe it should be."

"Curiosity has given us medicine...art...civilization itself."

"Curiosity gave us Agent Orange."

"Yeah, I suppose it did."

"Every choice is a prison."

"*Every choice is a prison.*"

"And every prison is a choice. Someone dreams it, someone builds it, someone dwells inside it."

"Why would we choose a cage, Emily?"

"Because it's safer than not choosing a cage."

"But you escaped."

"And escape is its own prison, I have discovered."

"The day that you saw Seth through the window, that was still some years ago. What brought you here now? What was your last day in the house?"

"Last day. They all bleed together."

"What lead up to your last day?"

"I can't."

"Yes, you can."

"Not now. It's too much."

"Just take it slow."

Follow; don't lead. But...nudge if you must.

"I really can't do this."

"I believe in you."
She sighed.
Finally…
"A young man came through the front door one day…"

Sour Meat, My Dear

A young man came through the front door one day. Very young. So handsome. So tall and lean.

"Hello?" he said, all twangy and yummy and new. "Anybody home? What's the deal with this here house anyhow, huh?"

Emily and I both wanted him right away.

"Hi there! Welcome! We are so glad you're here!"

"Two of yuh? Is y'all twins?"

"HA HA HA HA HA HA HA HA HA HA!!! You are so SILLY!"

"What's y'alls' names?"

"It doesn't matter anymore."

"Wutchoo mean it don't matter?"

"Please, come in! Come in!"

Oh, he was such a pretty young man. Although I suppose you might say he wasn't really a man, right? More like a boy? We had a good 22 years on him, probably. Maybe more than that. Still, he was a tall boy. And strong. Tall for thirteen anyway.

We wanted him so bad. We had to get him upstairs. To the circle room. It was so easy to get him up there. Didn't have to drag him, didn't have to drug him. So easy.

It was so easy to have them both. Any way we wanted. The two of them took to the house like they had been born to be there. Never the fear. Never the longing for outside. Never the homesickness. Never barricaded themselves in their room. Not alone, anyway. Of course, Emily and I made it worth their time. It is a funny thing...it really makes me giggle...I suppose that if we had done that out here, we would have been locked *away in prison for life. It is a crazy world.*

The four of us, we were pretty well...intertwined for the next several weeks. They were so delicious, those boys. They liked the dark things. The deep down...deep down...Oooohhhh...no...I really, really don't think I can do this right now.

"Yes, you can."

"I...I think I'm...having anxiety."

"Keep going."

"Let's just take a break, okay?"

"And talk about what?"

"So, okay, so...we were all exploring some...some more off-the-beaten...Ohhh..."

"Just try to settle down, Emily."

Emily began to shiver. Her right hand was outside the down comforter, and she flapped her fingers toward her face.

"Please, let's stop."

"No."

"Please!"

"No."

"It was...it was an afternoon," she said, breathing harder. "Emily and me and the two tall boys..."

"All of thirteen."

"They were strong."

"Good."

"There were... they liked... chains."

"Chains?"

"Thick, steel chains. They liked those."

"Did they now?"

"So heavy, Emily and I could barely lift them. But the boys, they loved the chains."

"What's the appeal?"

"They tie you up, they pin you down...they're cold. They hurt. They loved how it hurt."

"The house had steel chains?"

"Of course. Doesn't yours?"

"Probably."

"So... intense..."

"Fantastic. Go on."

"We were... downstairs... living room... we were, you know..."

"The four of you."

"The four of us. The boys were... excited—I can't!"

"Yes, you can."

"I can't do this right now!"

"Yes, you can."

"Okay...the one, the boy with Emily, he was too excited. Hot and sweaty. His muscular back nicked and welted by heavy chain links." I saw that her right hand had slipped back inside the blanket. "He was on top of her, going too fast. Pumping and pumping away. *Oh god...*He finished too quickly. Way too soon. She laughed at him. We laughed at him. He was embarrassed."

"It happens."

It happens...

"But the boy on top of me, *oh no, oh no,* he was g-going, going strong..."

"I want more detail."

"Um... it was good... it was, *uh*, nice..."

"That's not detail."

She was flustered, quivering. "Harder and harder..."

Movement within the blanket intensified.

"That's better."

"It was *huh huh* so good," she said, panting. "*Huuuuhhh...* It feels—it felt so good."

"Mm hm."

"So *uhhh...* so good..."

"Okay."

"I was about to come... *oh god...* I... *uuuuuhhh...* no no no... I was *no no no no no*... I was about to come so hard... I don't think... I can, *uh*..."

The blanket flapped ever more urgently.

"Don't stop now, Emily."

"Wh-... when suddenly, *oooooohh*... the other boy... he attacked him!"

"YES!"

"Knocked him right off of me! They went at each other with the chains swinging and smashing! So much screaming Oh GOD! OH GOD!!! So much blood! Blood everywhere! Blood all over us!!! Oh god, look away from me! LOOK AWAAAAAAAAAAAAY!!!"

Like a gentleman, I turned my head away as she arched her back, convulsing so hard the sofa shook. She squealed and moaned.

"Ooooh... ooooooooooooooh..." she cooed, gasping for breath and quaking. "Oh god... I'm sorry..."

"Don't be sorry."

"I couldn't help myself... I couldn't... I couldn't help it... I just needed to come..."

"It's fine, Ms. Conlin."

"Please don't—*gasp*—please don't put this in the book," she said, shuddering.

"I won't," I lied.

"Those boys... those fucking boys..."

"What did you and Emily do?"

"What do you mean?"

"I mean, what did you do?"

"We held each other and watched. Wouldn't you?"

"You didn't try to stop them?"

"It wasn't our business to meddle in their affairs."

"And then?" She didn't answer, still whimpering in post-orgasmic aftershock. "And then?!"

"And then nothing," she said finally, tiny as a church mouse. "They killed each other." Pause. "Their beautiful faces smashed into meat and gristle. Their gorgeous bodies ripped apart. Blood everywhere."

"We are all just meat and gristle anyway. It happens."

"Everyone in the house blamed us. Of course. *'This is your mess,'* she growled in a deep, manly voice, *'you stupid fuckin' twats. You mop it up!'* And so, we mopped it up. We tried to. We had never had to deal with bodies before. Plenty of death in the house, but never our responsibility. Plenty of death. The bodies have to go somewhere. It had never been our job until then.

"We didn't bother to get dressed. Why soil outfits? We scrubbed the floors. We scrubbed the rugs. We got bloodier and bloodier, but the room never got clean. Not completely. Blood caked in the cracks of the hardwood floor. We wrapped the boys in quilts and the blood soaked through. Soaking us." Emily put on a calm, matronly voice I took to be the woman in the white blouse. *"'You need to dispose of them, sweeties. It's such a shame they are dead now. They were quite lovely.'"*

"Dispose of them," I said.

"The bodies had to go somewhere," she said. "Shall we go down to the cellar? Now? To the cold storage?"

"I can't wait."

She stood up, dropping the blanket to the floor of the deck. A cold wind shook the treetops.

"It had to be done, but…They were too heavy to carry. We had to drag them by their feet down the wood staircase to the cellar. Their heads hit each step. Thump… thump… thump. Blood seeped through every layer of quilt. Trail of red all the way down. Even before we got to the cold storage, the cellar was painfully cold. And we were naked. Drenched in blood. Our bare feet nearly froze to the cellar floor, sticking with each step. I… don't… I…"

"We don't stop here, Emily."

She paced about the deck. In the distance, the first inkling of sunrise made its presence known.

"We dragged and dragged them," she said, looking about the

deck, but seeing some other space in her mind. "The red trail following our every step. Every inch they seemed to grow heavier, like they were gathering gravity as we went. Finally, past the wine rack, we reached the door...pulled up on the handle...and..."

"Yes?" Pause. "Yes?"

"The stench was an assault. Even at that temperature, you could taste the rot and death. It hung in the air. We collapsed to the floor heaving, she and I." Emily fell to her knees onto the hard, wooden deck. I continued writing. "My stomach forcing its way up my throat. Hers the same, I'm sure. We sobbed and retched."

"You have a job to do, Emily," I said. "Do your goddamn job."

"I can't get up off the floor!" she cried.

"Yes, you can."

"I'm frozen! I'm empty!"

"Get up."

Slowly, she stood.

"I stood first. I stood first to face it. Face the death. Emily remained on her knees, vomiting and shaking. There they were in piles. In stacks. Backs and ribs like washboards. Dead soles of cold feet. Wide, empty eyes. Fingers twisted into frozen hooks like talons. Faces. Faces. Some in pairs, some alone. Cold and dark and all death...but it was a bright, sunny day outside."

In the east, the sun cracked the tree line.

Serendipity.

"How do you know?" I asked.

"Yes, how."

"How did you know?"

"At the far-right end of the room was a standard basement window: thick safety glass and a vent shaft. I could see the sun shining through it. Because a section of the glass was broken out. Broken out...broken out...broken out..."

"Was Emily still on the floor?"

"She was just beginning to stand when I made my move. I

planted my left foot on some cold, stiff neck and I launched myself on top of the pile. Combat crawling across decades of forgotten and discarded husks, I headed toward to the sunlight. I didn't look back."

"And Emily?"

"She screamed, 'Emily, what are you doing?! Stop it! Come back!' I didn't stop, I crawled faster. 'EMILY! EMILY! STOP!' I did not look back. I never looked back. Lest I turned to stone, or salt, or was dragged back down forever. Her screaming grew closer, 'Emily, please!!!' She was crawling too. Chasing me. I crawled faster. Her screaming grew closer. I reached the broken safety glass and slammed against it with my bare shoulder. I heard a crack, and I did not know if it was glass or bone. I didn't care. I slammed again. I slammed again. Her screaming grew closer, 'EMILY, DON'T LEAVE US! DON'T LEAVE US ALONE!' I smashed the glass bricks through and slid out head-first into the waiting grass, feeling for one brief second her fingers grasping at my blood-slick toes. I pulled myself up and ran back to Down Pattersons. I tried to scream for help, but no sound would come out. Sharp stones and thorns slashed my soft feet. Scream and scream and nothing but wheezing air." She turned around to look at me, the morning sunlight cast all about her, her eyes dark like marbled midnight. "It is… a… it's a blur after that," she said. "Someone found me, someone cleaned me, someone dressed me, someone fed me. Someone tended to my wounds. Someone knew to call Seth. A day or so later, he came to pick me up. And that… is how I came to be here with you now."

We looked at each other in silence. The first of the morning birds began to call and sing.

"So you left her there," I said, finally. "Emily Conlin, naked and bloody on a heap of corpses."

"I saw my opportunity, and I grabbed it." Pause. "Wouldn't you?"

I stood up and stretched. I tucked my small spiral notebook and pen back into my jacket pocket.

Okay.

All right.

Only one thing left to do now.

"I don't know," I said. I inhaled deeply, then exhaled. "I couldn't wager a guess. So, we are going to have to find out."

"W—what?" she gasped. "What do you mean?"

"I like this story, Emily. I like it a lot. But there are... gaps. Gaps I don't think you are in any state to fill. I think our story needs some impartial field research."

"You... you can't be serious!" she exclaimed. "You just can't be!"

"I can be serious."

I turned and walked into the cabin. The fire had burned to ash and embers, glowing orange and dimming down. She followed me inside.

"This is MY story!"

As I passed through the kitchen toward the main room, I tapped the panic button on the underside of the counter. "I agree," I said. "Right now it is. And I really think, to really make this sucker pop, it needs to be *our* story."

"You can't go in there!" she cried. "It's suicide!"

"Or murder," I said, quickly packing my book bag and duffle. "If there is indeed a difference."

"Please don't! You go in there, and you will not come out!"

"I think I will. I'm pretty sure. But I am definitely sure I need to see it for myself."

I moved toward the door. She walked toward me urgently.

"I'll do better," she said, pleading, her hands folded. "I will do a better job of being descriptive. I've just... I have never done this before."

"You did a fine job, Emily. I like the story just fine. There are just some things I need to check out to do this thing justice."

"You don't understand. I was in there for twenty years. How long do you think we have for you to go find yourself?!"

"How long? What is time? Time is eternal. You said that."

"Listen to me. The number of occupants in that house is constantly in flux, and yet almost no one ever gets out. What does that tell you?"

"That weak people are often destroyed by their need for a cage. But I'm not worried. I have never been particularly taken by the comfort of confined spaces."

"You'll ruin everything."

"I'm just going as an observer, okay?"

"That's absurd! You won't be able to resist it!"

"You underestimate me."

"You overestimate yourself!"

"That is what I do."

"You can't avoid it. You cannot avoid the circle room. No one can. Everyone meets themselves in there eventually."

"I won't." I pulled out my phone and dialed 911. They answered, asking about my emergency. "I'm leaving," I told them.

"NO!" she shouted. "Don't fucking come here!"

"She's not safe here alone, so please hurry," I said into the phone and hung up. "I'll call Seth on my way."

"I will send them after you," she spat. "I'll tell them you did all kinds of things to me here last night."

"No, you won't. You want this book just as badly as I do. Probably more."

"You don't know what I want. You have no idea. You could never know."

I nodded and walked out the front door.

"Thank you very much for the gripping yarn, Emily. I'll be seeing you."

"I doubt I'll be seeing you," she said, following me to the front part of the porch. I jumped down the steps and threw my bags in the back seat of my car. "There are other writers, you know. I don't have to wait for you!"

"One way or another, I'm walking out of there with the definitive text," I said. "I would have to think that you'd rather be a part of that than some cheap knock-off. Always be proud of that which bears your name, Emily." I opened the driver-side door and got in.

"I've read your books," she said, her face scrunched, her eyes red and watery. "I have seen what you do to your characters. I don't want to be one of your characters."

"You already are, my dear." I turned on the ignition and blew her a kiss. "Some sunny day."

I put the car in reverse and backed out onto the road. She ran down the steps into the sharp gravel of the carport.

"IF SHE'S DEAD!" she screamed at me as she shrank smaller and smaller in my rearview mirror. "If she's dead... I DON'T WANT TO KNOW!!!"

THE DUPLICATION HOUSE: PARLOR

[Pages fed through a crack in the glass]

Thursday: 11am. Drinking Jack Daniel's in Malibu Al's Beach Bar at LAX reading Dostoevsky's *Notes from Underground.* "I have to say, it's pretty damn good, Sal," I told my agent on the phone. "I can see why it was so popular with the Beat Generation." I was glad he called. "Hard to believe it has taken me this long to read it." It had not been a great week up to that point. "I don't think I'll need to read it twice, though." But an actual phone call from your lit agent? That is typically a positive sign. Forward momentum.

"I always thought it was called *Notes from THE Underground,*" he said.

"Yeah, that's what I had thought too," I said, looking at the front cover. It was the Bantam Classics edition. "But nope."

"Well, I'll be damned. I could have sworn the title on the Dover Thrift ed—"

"Sat behind Henry Winkler on the flight in."

"Oh yeah? The Fonz himself."

"I recognized him, but come to think of it, I can't remember the last thing I actually saw him in."

"He's on a show now. Pretty good. It's about a lovable hitman. He is not the hitman, though."

"Ah, the old *lovable hitman-aroo.* Classic."

"I know, it's gross. But they actually do it well. You should check it out."

"I don't watch TV."

"And yet, there you are in LA, pitching scripts."

"A script. Singular."

"How did the meeting go?"

I finished my Jack on the rocks and contemplated another.

"It was a goddamn disaster. An absolute, apocalyptic shit tornado."

"Fuck. Sorry to hear it, man," he said. "It is a good piece. A gripping yarn and all. Everybody knows it's good. That's why Marsha agreed to represent you. Just not commercial is all."

"I've got friends winning awards, Sal," I said. "ALL the awards. *New York Times* best sellers. Meanwhile, I couldn't sell a damn kidney, let alone a manuscript."

"Hopefully, you are treating your scripts better than you treat your kidneys."

That last drink started to hit me. "Fair point, Sally." I decided to order a screwdriver. For the vitamins. "An entirely fair point."

"How are your classes going? Do your fellow students even know who you are?"

I had to laugh. "Who I am? Who *am* I?"

I'm dirty, mean, mighty unclean, I'm a wanted man.

"Have you talked to you-know-who since you've been in LA?" Sal asked me.

"We texted a bit last night," I replied, "but no. I haven't seen her. Her pilot is set to air, though, from the sound of it."

"Good. Good for her. You love to hear about a solid win."

"Absolutely. She deserves it."

"So...I'm thinking," he said, "you should probably take this ghost-writing gig, yeah?"

I thought about my last night in Cali. There was nothing interesting going on around the hotel where I was staying. There weren't even any bars nearby, which was good because I was nearly out of money, anyway. I spent the last of it on a bottle of Wild Turkey, a pinch of smoke, and a full-size tube of toothpaste I was going to have to throw away at the airport because it might be a bomb. Of course.

I was certain that I wouldn't be able to sleep. I flipped on the TV in time to see a friend of mine being featured on that HBO show about fucking. I had known her primarily as a playwright, and a damn good playwright at that. And she also did sex work, it seemed. This was news to me. She was really going at it on HBO with another gal and a real muscular dude. Turned it off. Like I told Sal, I just don't really care for television.

Out of the blue, I got a rather odd melody in my head. I don't write music much anymore. I don't even own a guitar anymore, sadly enough, as I had hawked the last one for rent money. But, as I sat there in my dingy hotel room staring at the nicotine-yellow wallpaper, something that sounded like a song started developing in my brain. I wrote down the melody and chord progression in my notebook (E with an A sympathetic drone, D# to G#). And then, without giving it much thought, lyrics of some sort began to form. I wrote them down as they arrived.

Leering through the clearing field
Nearly keeping sealed in fear
Old, the morning dear
Fear it, keep it sealed in steel

"The fuck?" I said out loud to my spiral notebook as it lay spread open on the hotel room bedcover. I looked at the words but could not place them in any particular context. Apart from matching the melody, I could not fathom what any of it might mean...to the degree that *meaning* is in any way essential.

Hold the moon, my dear
Steal it, clearly feeling healed
Praise it happening as often
Scream and scrape the lid of my coffin

"That doesn't help," I said aloud to the alien stanzas in my notebook.

Hold the moon my dear...
Hold the moon my dear...
Hold the moon my dear...

Hold the moon my dear…

I closed my notebook and tossed it to the floor. *That's enough of that for now.*

I heard the text alert on my phone go *wmp wmp wmp.* Checked the screen. It was *her.*

> *R U still in town?*—she asked.
> *No*—I lied.
> *Boo.*—
> *How's your pilot going?*—
> *It's going.*—
> *That's good.*—
> *Miss U kinda*—
> *I miss you too.*—

I flipped on the TV again in time to see a lion tearing into a cape buffalo. Flipped it off again. It was only 2 am, but I knew I should probably try to snag some winks since I had to fly out before too long. Thankfully, I was a little high. I closed my eyes, and…what was it that Jonathan Harker said? Something about "all sorts of queer dreams?" I have those.

"What is the guy's name, Sal? The guy who called you."

"Seth Conlin. It's not about him, though. You wouldn't really be dealing with him that much. It's his sister. Emily, I think her name is."

"She was the missing person?"

"Twenty years. Then, after all that time, she turns up naked in the forest near their childhood home caked in blood."

"That is…quite a thing."

"Do you want me to connect you?"

"I don't know. What do you think?"

"It sounds right up your alley to me."

"In truth, I cannot disagree with that."

"Your call, man."

"We actually gonna sell this one, Sally? Or is it just another speck of dust?"

"We could insist on a flat up front, then negotiate a royalty split after we find a publisher."

"Will we find a publisher?"

"Yeah, I think so. Probably. Maybe."

"Okay...so...Where am I heading?"

"West Virginia."

"I can't wait."

Wheeling and Dealing

I met Seth Conlin at a little neighborhood bar on Warwood Ave. on the outskirts of Wheeling, West Virginia.

"Jack on the rocks, yes?" he said, handing me a tumbler. Very handsome. Not that he's my type or anything, but you have to admire a fine specimen when you see one in the wild.

"Mr. Conlin, I presume." We clinked glasses, and he led me over to a booth in the corner.

"How was your flight in?"

"I flew into Ohio and picked up my car there," I told him. "The drive was nice enough. The flight was a bit of a hell ride. I was seated right next to this catastrophically drunk woman who barfed into a paper bag the *entire flight*!"

"Oh, shit!" Seth guffawed.

"The *WHOLE* flight, dude!" I said, exaggerating my gesticulations. "Right before take-off I saw her ping-ponging down the aisle and I'm like, *Please don't sit this trifling bitch next to me.* Welp, sure enough!" Seth laughed like he hadn't done so in quite a while. His face was as red as a ripe tomato. It was kind of adorable. "Seriously, who the fuck drinks that much before a flight?! Well, except for me. But I can handle my shit, goddamn it!"

"HA HA HA HA HA HA!!!"

"She filled three fuckin' bags! Meanwhile, I'm leaning half out into the aisle getting struck by service carts going both ways."

"Livin' the dream, my friend," Seth said, wiping his eyes on a paper napkin. "Livin' the damn dream."

"Every damn day."

"Sorry to laugh at your misery, man, but hell."

"Right?! At least I had a decent book to read."

"What were you reading?"

"Dostoevsky."

"*Crime and Punishment*? That is one of my favorites!"

"So yeah, all things considered, no complaints."

"Cheers!"

We clinked glasses again, and a waitress brought over another round of drinks I did not recall ordering. We ordered some hotdogs as well, because why not.

"So, Seth," I said, downing my first drink and moving on to my second. "I hate to be drab and official right from the get-go, and I don't know what Mr. Willis has told you about this sort of thing, but my standard flat is $7500, which, believe me, is insanely cheap. Sal would shop it, of course. In the event of a sale, fingers crossed, we split the advance in half. All royalties are sixty/forty. I have an okay relationship with a couple of publishers right now. If one of them picks it up, we will need to renegotiate a separate contract on e-sales and audio recordings, should you even decide to go with the latter. The former is a given, of course."

"That all sounds totally fine," he said. "I don't know if we should get too ahead of ourselves, though. You haven't even met Emily yet. You might change your mind. I wouldn't blame you a bit if you did."

For reasons I still cannot fully understand even now, hearing him say her name out loud gave me a slight shudder. It was as if he had mentioned a ghost.

"How is your sister these days?" I asked. "How are you both doing? It must be difficult."

Seth smiled, warm but a bit strained. He had very pretty teeth. "We do okay," he said. "We do okay. Em and me, we didn't really know our dad growing up. I didn't know him at all. Him and Mama, they split up when Emily was ten and I was two. I remember meeting him once, maybe, but fuck, it might not even be a real memory, you know? He moved to Knoxville at some point. Got killed on the highway driving a commercial truck. Mama got some money from it, which I got when Mama passed a few years ago." Pause. "It was hard, you know. It was real hard. I was all alone, pretty much still a kid. But we do okay."

"Sounds hard, man."

"I mean, don't get me wrong. It is amazing to have her back in my life again after all this time. It's just... It's wild, I'll tell you what."

"Where is Emily now?"

"I've got a cabin out on Rock Lake about an hour and a half from here. Nine acres, right on the waterfront, no neighbors to speak of. Wheeling ain't exactly Tokyo, you understand, but there is still a bit too much hustle and bustle for her just yet."

"But she was found close to where you grew up, right? Near your hometown?"

"Barely even a town really," he chuckled. "I don't know what you'd call it exactly. But yeah, that's where they found her."

"After twenty years?"

"Twenty years, nearly to the day, if my memory is at all truthful."

"So... you had not seen her since you were in, what, second grade? Do you even remember her?"

"I mean..." he replied, trailing off.

"I can barely remember people I dated a few years ago, let alone someone I haven't seen since I was seven years old."

"We do okay," he said again. "We do okay."

"And the whole time nobody knew where she was?"

With that, Seth's demeanor shifted. His shoulders slumped like extra gravity had just landed on him. It seemed like a rather obvious question to me, but apparently, he was not adequately prepared for it.

"Oh...no..." he said, suddenly rather small. He looked down at his drink. The fingers on his left hand drummed against the table. "No, I knew exactly where she was."

"Um…" I said, more than a bit startled. "Waitaminute… What?"

"I was with her when she…"

"When she what, Seth?"

"Fuck… I don't… I don't know how to say this."

Our hot dogs arrived. I munched down on mine right away. It was quite good. Seth took maybe two bites of his.

"The hell are you talking about, Mr. Conlin?" I asked. "What sort of yarn are we spinning here?"

"I can't explain it," he whispered desperately, his voice and fingers trembling. "*You need to talk to Emily.*"

Emily Outside.

For an hour and a half, I followed Seth's taillights through the black of the West Virginia night. He gave me the address so I could GPS it, but he was correct when he told me it would try to take me down roads that have not been roads in quite a while.

The broken lines of the divider blipped by like an EKG. I tried to keep my eyes from succumbing to highway hypnotism. We did not stop once the entire time.

When we finally arrived at the cabin, I stepped out of the car and breathed in the crisp country air. Even in the dead of night, I could see the bucolic wonder of our surroundings: rolling acres of green, a tree-lined horizon, the moonlight shimmering across the still water of the lake. I grabbed my duffle and my book bag out of the back seat of my car.

Seth still seemed tense. The hour-and-a-half drive had clearly not calmed his nerves. "It would probably be best to ease Emily into this," he said quietly. "Don't push her. When she's ready, she'll talk. You are welcome to stay as long as you like. But if you feel the need to leave, you have no obligations as far as I'm concerned."

"Okay."

He put one boot on the bottom step, then paused. He turned to me and said, "It gets bad here at night sometimes."

"I hear ya."

And with that, we went in.

Inside the cabin was warm and comfortable. Twenty-five hundred square ft, natural, exposed woodwork, high ceilings, finished loft with private rooms, two bed, two bath, full kitchen, wrap-around porch that overlooks the lake, indoor and outdoor stone fireplaces. Quality.

"There's an extra room upstairs," Seth whispered. "It's my room when I'm here, usually, but you are welcome to it."

"The couch is fine," I whispered in return.

We stood statue-still for a moment in perfect silence. Not a peep.

Seth's face finally began to relax.

Suddenly, we heard a piercing wail from upstairs.

"Fuuuuck," he groaned, and ran upstairs. I heard the rattling of a doorknob. "Em! It's me! Open the door!" More hysterical shrieking. "Move the bureau away from the door! Em, it's just ME, goddamn it!"

I heard furniture scraping across hardwood floor, and a door flying open. I could not see what was going on, but I heard muffled sobbing. Then I heard the door shut, and then *mostly* silence again.

Whatever. It's all the same to the clam.

I plopped down onto the sofa and cashed out. Queer nightmares galore.

It was still dark when I felt myself being nudged awake.

'*But why sleep?*' I thought. '*You lie down on a sofa—and in a flash, sleep flies away.*'

"Hey," Seth whispered. "I gotta head on out."

'*Miles and miles away...*'

"Okay."

"She'll likely sleep into the day, but she will be up eventually."

Pause. "She'll be fine."

'So you rub your eyes, get up, and it starts all over again.'

"Worry not, Mr. Conlin," I said with a yawn. "All will be well."

So sayeth Jean-Paul.

He smiled, looking at least somewhat relieved. I really liked his smile.

"I appreciate ya, sir," he said. We shook hands, and he departed.

The cabin was still. It was the most silence I had heard in quite some time. Through the window, I saw the top edge of the morning sun peeking up from behind the trees. I snorted a little morning bump and grabbed a breakfast Guinness from the bar's mini-fridge, then headed outside to greet the dawn.

The frost on the grass crunched under my boots as I walked toward the lake. Fog rolled up the hill over the short stone retaining wall as the sun tossed a sheet of blood orange across the rippling water. I took a hearty belt of Guinness and inhaled the country air, a bit of chemical glaze dripping down the back of my throat. *This is living.*

I sat down on the wall and pulled a pen and notebook out of my bookbag.

> On September 4, 1896, Antoine "Antonin" Artaud was born in Marseilles, France. From the very beginning, Artaud's life was filled with pain and anguish. Of his eight siblings, six died young. The death of his infant sister Germaine at the hands of an abusive nanny when Artaud was nine also haunted him throughout his life (Eshleman 2). The chronic sickness, family turmoil, and perpetual mental and emotional degradation of Artaud's daily existence both fed and

challenged his creative vision. Arguably one of the most influential figures in the history of Western theatre, Antonin Artaud first came to prominence as a writer within the French Surrealist movement while working with a number of experimental theatre collectives in Paris during the 1920s. From very early on, Artaud struggled against the performative and emotive limitations of the written word and hoped to create an approach to theatre where language would be overshadowed by sound and spectacle, where the director's vision, not the script, would create the architecture of the play. When political infighting resulted in his parting ways with the surrealists, Artaud founded The Alfred Jarry Theatre, along with fellow surrealist writers Robert Aron and Roger Vitrac, with the hopes of radically transforming French theatre. The kind of theatre Artaud envisioned would only draw from "the classics" after they had been radically reimagined. Artaud's greatest contribution to Western theatre is, of course, his conception of the Theatre of Cruelty. Themes of rape, torture, degradation, defilement, and nightmarish violence are also part and parcel of the Theatre of Cruelty, which called for, as Martin Esslin describes, "a ruthless exposure of the deepest conflicts of the human mind" (334), and Albert Bermel called "a tragic, repulsive, impassioned farce, a marvelous wellspring for speculation, and a unique contribution to the history of drama" (20). By confronting its audience with the "true image of their internal conflicts," Esslin continues, "a poetic, magical theatre would bring liberation and release" (334). In a sense, then, in his assaults on theatrical conventions and audience expectations Artaud's work may be considered a more forceful challenge to the societal *status quo* than that of the later absurdist playwrights Beckett and Genet.

Not too bad. Could be a little funnier.

Artaud spent nine of his last eleven years confined within psychiatric institutions, but continued to write, though mostly preferring to write poetry over anything theatrical or theoretical. On March 4th, 1948, having been diagnosed with bowel cancer just two months prior, Artaud overdosed on chloral hydrate, and died alone.

*Hmmm...*I thought. *Still use some work.*

"*Toute écriture est de la merde de porc,*" said Artaud. "People who leave the obscure and try to define whatever it is that goes on in their heads are pigs."

Yes! NOW we're getting somewhere!
Feeling eyes upon me, I turned around. The space between the house and the lake was a bit greater than I had initially realized. Standing on the back porch of the cabin, I saw the figure of a woman in gray. It was Emily. Outside. She waved. I waved back.

I entered the cabin to the smell of eggs cooking and the sound of Nat 'King' Cole.
"*And when I grow too old to dream / I'll have you to remember / and when I grow too old to dream / your love / will*

live / in my heart…"

"Hey there!" I heard a bright, sing-songy voice float from the kitchen. It was the same voice I had heard shrieking the previous night, but considerably more cheerful.

"Emily?"

From around the corner came a woman in her early-to-mid thirties, if I were guessing, wearing her usual around-the-house outfit.

"Yes! Hi! Yes, that's me! How are you?" She walked over to me, and we shook hands.

"I'm well, thanks."

"Hungry?"

"Sure."

"I am sooooooo sorry about last night," she said. "It's so embarrassing. I just get really disoriented these days when I wake up in the night alone."

"It's fine, Ms. Conlin."

"Yikes. Weird. Let's just go with Emily, okay?"

"Emily it is."

She scooped the eggs onto two plates, squeezed out tea bags into ceramic mugs and tossed them in the trash. She danced a bit from counter to counter as she worked, humming along to the music. She was pretty, like Seth. You could certainly tell they were siblings.

"Should we eat outside? It is such a beautiful morning, after all."

"Sure," I said again.

I grabbed the plates, she grabbed the teas, and we headed out to the back deck.

We sat, watching hawks fly over the water and occasionally swoop down to grab something out of the lake.

"Were you writing a school paper down there on the retaining wall?" she asked me, her mouth half-filled with eggs.

"Yeah, I decided to go back. I have a degree in English already, but I felt like that probably wasn't enough, you know? So, we're trying Humanities."

"Humanities? What's that?"

"I don't really know how to explain it. It's basically the study of the things humans create."

"But isn't that, like, everything?"

"Yeah...I suppose it is."

"Would that include theatre?" she asked. She took a sip of her tea and winced like it had burned her. She blew on it and took a lighter sip. I took a drink of mine. It didn't seem all that hot to me.

"It would indeed. In fact, my current project is very theatre-centric, specifically the Theatre of the Absurd and the Theatre of Cruelty."

"Theatre of Cruelty. Wow."

"Yep. Good ol' Antonin Artaud."

"I have never heard of him."

"Artaud's creative talents were developed, in no small part, as a form of therapy during his many hospitalizations for various mental illnesses, which were exacerbated by prodigious drug abuse. During these times of hospitalization and drug abuse, he would declare himself a believer in God, then would curse religion and declare *himself* God. The body horror that was indelible to the Theatre of Cruelty and is on full display in *The Spurt of Blood* became an abiding obsession for Artaud during this time, as was his growing disgust with human sexuality."

"*The Spurt of Blood*?" she said. "That sounds like something *you* would write!"

"Agreed!" I said. "I have long suspected that Artaud ripped me off, despite the fact that he died exactly thirty years before I was born. No-good thievin' time-travelin' bastard." That was a really stupid joke, but it made Emily snort-laugh, which made me laugh too. "*The Spurt of Blood*," I continued, "is a fascinating oddity within the realm of dramatic theory. As an exploration of what is possible on stage, the 'play' deliberately confronts the limitations of the medium by requiring stage effects that even in the 21st century are not feasible, to say nothing of the depravity of the content itself. As a means of exorcizing his frustrations within his chosen medium, Artaud's *The Spurt of Blood* also serves as a challenge to all who hope to push theatre beyond what is often considered to be its boundaries. After all, since any attempt to stage *The Spurt of Blood* is destined to not succeed, even a modestly ambitious failure is sure to be compelling to witness."

"How come?" she asked. "Why is it destined to fail?"

"Well," I said, "if we are to be perfectly truthful, *every* endeavor is destined to fail, eventually. It's the very nature of things."

"Yeah, all right."

"But specifically, Artaud's stage directions for this insanely short—like four-page—play consist of effects that are impossible to achieve on stage: earthquakes, severed limbs falling progressively more slowly from the rafters, on-stage incest, breasts turning into cheese, a giant hand grabbing a woman whose hair catches fire while the wrist of the hand hemorrhages blood across the stage, a swarm of scorpions bursting forth from under a woman's dress which attack a man's genitals, and so on. *The Spurt of Blood* has never been a practical work of theatre but is a noble conceptual experiment all the same."

"I'm not going to lie," she said, "that sounds delightful."

"I one hundred percent concur. A *theatre of cruelty* would be a theatre of flesh and blood, theatre in its rawest, most primitive form, devoid of intellectualization, devoid of civility, devoid of socialization, devoid of any external, socially imposed ethics or morality. This would be a theatre of imagination in its purest form, devoid of all constructed morality."

"I used to love theatre back when I was in school. I played Rita in my high school's production of *Prelude to a Kiss*."

"Ah yes, Craig Lucas. Nice one! That is a pretty racy show for tenth graders. Isn't that the last time you were in school? 9th or 10th grade?"

She looked down at her plate in silence, shoveling eggs into her mouth.

Shit, I thought. *I hope I didn't just trigger something. But hell, this is why we're here, right?*

"Do you like theatre?" she asked, a bit more subdued than before. "Or is it just an academic thing for you?"

"I do like it. Anything *Cruel* and/or *Absurd* is right up my alley."

"Cruel and absurd," she echoed, sipping her tea. "I wouldn't know anything about that." I could have sworn she was being sarcastic, but I could not be quite certain. I also wasn't sure if I should ask her questions, or just let her tell me whatever she wanted to.

Follow; don't lead.

Finally, she said, "I noticed you also write a lot about bloody stuff. Like your guy Antoine, or whatever."

"Um...yeah. I guess I do."

"A lot of blood. "

"Yep."

"Blood and screwing."

"I hadn't thought of it quite that way, but yeah."

"You are definitely the best choice for this job."

All right, that's a start. I think.

"Well," I said. "I'm here. And my arsenal, such as it is, is at your disposal."

"Okay, thanks."

"So...what can you tell me about *the house?*"

"Well...it's haunted."

"Oh yeah? Ghosts, huh? That's an angle."

"No, not by ghosts."

"By whom?"

"By me. Among others."

Hmmmm...

"All right."

"No one ever went in there; nobody I ever saw. But from

what was understood, more people went in than came out." Pause. "This was before my time, or when I was just an infant maybe, but some lady went in there. The only certified librarian in the town's history, apparently. Her son had gone missing in the woods. Went creeking alone, I guess, and never came home. Probably fell into the Pattersons and was washed away—it happens. Everybody pretty much knew he was dead and long gone, but she was convinced he was in that house. So, she went after him, and was missing for two months. When she finally came stumbling back into town one day, from what I heard, she was in really bad shape. Cut up and beaten, wrists all torn up and bloody. Pretty much catatonic from then on, I suppose."

"Never found him, huh?"

"Nope."

"Damn," I said, writing all of that down in my notebook. "You think she is still in town?"

"No idea," she said. "Like I said, that was before my time. I highly doubt it, though." Pause. "If we kids ever got too nosy, we would be given just the barest of facts. 'Just stay away from that house.' That's all they would ever tell us. And everybody did. Just went about their days pretending the house wasn't out there, tangled in among the brambles and briars."

"*Nearly* everybody."

"I have always been a curious girl."

"What does the house look like?"

"Old," she said. "Of course. Rickety. Charred and smoky, where people had tried to burn it down and failed. The windows are busted out. On the outside. It looks empty and bare. From the outside. We never heard a sound from within. Not a peep. Not a creak. Which made the sudden random appearance of a screaming, flailing, occasionally blood-soaked person busting out the front door all the more peculiar. It's not really something you want to get used to, but you would be surprised."

"We can get accustomed to an awful lot, I have noticed."

"True enough," she said. Pause. "Porch floorboards creaked

under my feet. For one split second, I thought twice about opening the front door, and just turning tail and running. But...instead...I stepped inside."

She got up and walked back into the cabin.

Whoa. Okay then...guess we are done out here for now.

I grabbed the dishes and followed her in.

"What did you see, Emily? What did you see when you walked inside?"

"I saw two figures, barely visible, not much but shadows. Two ladies. Older, but not old. Fifty-ish when I first met them. They were kind to me."

"Did you ask their names?"

"It doesn't matter anymore."

"It matters to me," I said, trying not to sound testy. "It matters to the story."

"They told me they wished nothing but the best for my sweet girl."

"Your sweet girl?"

"One of them did. The other didn't talk much. She didn't really talk at all. She never made much of a sound, even when she was taking it hard."

Pause.

Um...

"Let's...unpack that a bit, shall we?"

"No," Emily said. "I don't think so."

"Okay. What else did they say? What did she say, the one who talked?"

"They said that I should feel free to explore the entire house. And they said that the circle room awaits me upstairs when I'm ready."

"The circle room..."

"It's not really a circle, though. I don't know why we called it that."

"What else did they tell you?"

"They said just to be sure to avoid the cold storage deep in the back of the cellar."

"How come?"

She was silent for a few moments, then said, "Sour meat, my dear. You don't want a taste of that." Pause. "There was tea in the fridge. Someone had fixed a fresh batch of biscuits and marmalade. I had some. It was all right."

"Who did?" I asked. "Who prepared them?"

"It doesn't matter anymore."

"Who were those women, Emily?" I asked. Emily turned to look at me. I indicated that there was room on the couch. She declined, continuing to stand and pace.

"They were my friends," Emily said, small but direct.

"I sincerely doubt that."

"They were."

'In what ways were they your friends?"

"In what ways is anybody friends with anybody?"

"Did they ever hurt you?"

"No," she said. "Not once. Never."

"Did they touch you?"

"We touched each other."

Okay...here we go...

"Is that right?" I said, keeping my voice non-committal. I wrote down what she said in my notebook.

"There were men too. Men and women. We all touched each other."

"Did the men ever hurt you?"

"Only if I begged them too," she said. I got the sense just then, for the moment, that she no longer really considered me present. In the cabin. In her world. Anywhere. She was somewhere else.

"And how about the cellar. Did you check it out?"

"Yes...eventually..."

"Was it cold?"

"So...so cold..."

I should have noticed her trembling. I guess I chose not to notice.

"And the storage room?"

"Ohhhh…"

"Tell us about the cold storage, Emily."

Emily collapsed at the waist and screamed, banging herself on the head with her fist and pulling her own hair. I leapt off the couch and grabbed her, holding both her wrists to stop her from hurting herself. She fell into me, sobbing. I led her over to the couch and held her as she cried. It was very uncomfortable. *I am not trained for this.*

I wanted to leave. I wanted to walk away from this project. I should have. If I had the chance to do it all over again, I likely would.

Instead, we decided to have some wine, order Chinese delivery, and talk about something other than the house just north of Pattersons Creek for a while.

After dinner, we took a little stroll about the grounds. As we walked down the hill past the retaining wall, we saw a small wooden boat dock at the edge of the lake.

"Does Seth have a boat?" I asked.

"I don't actually know," she said. "I don't really come down here much." She stepped cautiously onto the dock, toward the lake's edge, and looked down into the water. She immediately backed away.

"You see something?"

"Let's go back," she said quickly.

"How come?"

"I'm not ready yet."

"Ready for what?"

"This is dangerous down here," she said, stepping off the dock and walking toward the hill.

"I can swim," I said. "I'll rescue you."

"No one can rescue me," she said. "It is way too late for that."

"I doubt it."

"Don't overestimate yourself," she said.

"That's what I do."

She chuckled dryly, and headed up the hill back to the cabin. "I'll bet." I followed her. About halfway up, she stopped and turned toward me. "I'm glad we're doing this book together. I really want to get this out of my head." She tapped herself on the forehead. I nodded. And then, apropos of not much, she said, "I think you are very kind."

"You think very wrong," I said.

"I doubt it," she said, echoing me. "I'm a good judge of character."

"That's good."

"But... I have seen what you do to your characters."

"Yeah?"

"You destroy them."

I nodded.

No *denying.*

We spent the rest of the evening on the back deck drinking wine. A lot of wine. She put Billie Holiday on the iPod. I put logs in the fireplace. Ash and pine, nice and dry. They went up quick, in a beautiful orange flame. It was a particularly chilly evening, but Emily only wore a long sweater and shorts. No hat, no shoes, but she did toss a wool scarf around her neck at least. I zipped my jacket up all the way. I was still cold.

"I heard you used to be a musician," she said.

"A long time ago," I said. "In another life. I almost feel like that was somebody different. Some other version of me."

"What kind of music did you play?"

"I mean...whatever kind of books I write, that's the sort of music I played I guess."

"Do you miss it?"

"I don't really miss things."

"What? What does that mean?"

"That lobe that most people have in their brains that enables them to miss things, to miss people, to think wistfully back on the past, I don't have that."

"Really? Damn. All I do is miss people. It's all I have ever done."

"I cannot relate."

"Wow."

"Seriously. I have no idea what that feels like."

"So, when somebody tells you they miss you, what do you say to them?"

"I tell them I miss them too. But it's a lie. I actually don't."

"That is so sad."

"Is it? For whom?"

"When this book is finished someday and we go our separate ways, you won't ever miss me?"

"Why go separate ways? Hell, why finish it? Maybe we'll just keep writing this book forever and ever."

We laughed.

[*Note: My timeline might be off here. I am not actually sure when this exchange happened. I currently do not have access to a calendar.*]

"I sure do miss people," she said. "I miss Seth right now, and he's only a few hours away. I miss my mom a lot. I even kind of miss my dad, but not really. I miss all my old friends from way back when. I know I will never see them again. And even if I did see them, they wouldn't be them anymore. They would be people I don't know."

I thought of asking her if she missed anyone from the house near Down Pattersons. I'm glad I did not.

We talked the night away, polishing off one bottle after another. At a certain point, I went and fetched a blanket from Seth's bed for her to wrap around herself. She claimed she was not cold, but seeing her in nothing but a crew-neck sweater was making *me* cold, so I insisted. She teased me about it. *Oh well.*

Emily did occasionally strike me as someone who wasn't quite sure how to behave like an adult. She was fidgety in a way that struck me as very adolescent in nature. Her posture, the cadence of her voice, the way she constantly fiddled with her plastic anklet and twisted her hair around her finger, she seemed younger than she was. But this was not simply a case of arrested development. I would come to discover that nothing with Emily was simple.

"Since we're working together, can I ask you about your books?"

"All the blood and screwing?" I asked.

"Specifically, yes."

"Go for it."

"I know you disagree, but you seem to me like basically a decent person."

"False, but okay."

"And yet you write indecent things. Why is that?"

"Ultimately," I replied, "the validity of a work's content will be decided by its audience: an audience that may very well change its mind about the work several times over. For although this work may be rough at times, harsh, dark, coarse, even vulgar, that does not *necessarily* mean that the intent was to be exploitive or gratuitous. But...perhaps it was. After all, when a main theme of a work of art is the human impulse toward atrocity and inhumanity, does it not stand to reason that it might cross the boundaries of *good taste*? And why should it not? Are not atrocities themselves gratuitous? Crossing boundaries is crucial, after all. Be it socially, politically, or artistically, crossing boundaries is the only means by which progress can occur. It seems unlikely that cautious, restrained art could ever be as impactful as the more so-called 'dangerous' sort."

"Okay, but I feel like you didn't really answer my question."

"It's because the imagination has no morality."

"What do you mean by that?"

"A person could be moral in and of herself, and she certainly well should be. But her imagination, if she is any kind of an artist, must be completely amoral. A moral imagination is a stifled imagination."

I could tell she was giving this some thought.

Finally, she said, "I am not a particularly moral person."

"Is that right? I would not have guessed that."

"I've done...things. Unforgivable things."

"Are we going to write about them?"

"That is why you're here." Pause. A few tears spilled lightly down her cheeks. "*I'm a monster*," she whispered.

"Are you really?"

"Yes," she sniffled. "I am. I most certainly am."

"Most of my heroes were monsters," I said. "It happens."

"Like who?" she asked, wiping her face against the sleeves of her sweater.

"Jean Genet comes to mind," I said.

"The playwright?"

She took a swig of wine from the bottle and handed it to me.

I took a drink and handed it back. "Among other things. He was a criminal. A lifelong thief and a pervert. It has long been held that Genet had no sense of right or wrong, but I disagree with that assessment. I think he understood them perfectly well, and *consciously chose evil* as his clear preference."

"That doesn't sound right," she said. "He supported good things, didn't he? Good causes? Good revolutions? He spoke out for the underdogs."

"That's what he claimed."

"You don't buy it?"

"There is seldom a one-to-one relationship between a work of art that advocates...or appears to advocate... for a change to the *status quo*, and that change happening as a direct result. Influence, after all, can come in a variety of forms. Sometimes change happens that an artist did not intend; sometimes a work will inspire change many generations after the artist has died. Art endures while times change, and emergent ideologies subvert and replace previously dominant ones. Thus, certain works of art can potentially speak to the zeitgeist of a new generation as well, if not better, than the audience the artist had originally considered. Art is essential to the larger dialogue as it articulates facets of the human experience we are likely aware of, but had not fully considered, at least within the context in which it appears in the work. Art can also be willfully chaotic and deliberately obscure. Genet was all of that."

"That's fair I guess."

"But really, at the end of the day, it was only violence that got his dick hard."

"Violence..."

"Genet just liked to fuck vicious, bloodthirsty men," I said. "Or to be fucked by them." Pause. "But hey, who doesn't, right?" I looked over to her. She took another sizable gulp of wine but did not respond. Instead, she stared out at the lake.

"Genet didn't subvert society's conceptions of morality," I continued, "he opted to not acknowledge the society's morality at all. His work openly glories in death, perversion and annihilation. It celebrates murder as intrinsically positive, and inherently sexy. Crime is praised for its own sake, kindness is likely false and deserving of punishment, and prison is preferable to freedom because it is where evil lives and thrives."

"Plus, there's good screwing in prison," she said. I don't think she was joking, but I could not quite tell.

"Yes," I said, "from Genet's perspective, prison presented an opportunity for transgressive sexual adventure. However, having been to jail myself a few times, I must respectfully disagree."

"Respectfully," she replied, "prison and jail are two different things."

Touché.

"Have you read *Deathwatch*?"

"No, tell me about it."

"There are three prisoners—Green Eyes, Lefranc, and Maurice. They share a cell and await Green Eyes' execution. Because Lefranc and Maurice committed lesser crimes, and Green Eyes is a murderer, Green Eyes is clearly placed in a position of power and high regard, despite the fact that he is chained to the floor and is soon to be killed. Maurice and Lefranc vie for his attention. Both want to fuck him and are envious of the respect they assume he has garnered for his crime. They also lust after another inmate called Snowball, who is referenced but never introduced. They actually just want to fuck Snowball because he's Black. Anyway, in the end, Lefranc strangles Maurice to death in order to impress Green Eyes and have him all to himself. However, Lefranc's murder of Maurice arouses nothing but scorn in Green Eyes. Because nothing means anything forever."

"I love that," she said. "I would really like to read that sometime."

"Then you would really enjoy *The Maids*. I actually have that one with me. The play opens with Claire and Solange, two sisters who are handmaidens to a wealthy woman known only as Madame, playing dress-up. In keeping with the absurdist tradition of exploiting the intrinsic artifice of theatre and disrupting the audience's expectations, the reality of this role-playing game is not immediately evident. Instead, we are led to believe that what we are watching is Madame and Claire in Madame's boudoir on a typical day, wherein Madame dominates and humiliates Claire in a way that is, while not explicitly sexual, not particularly *subtle* either.

"'Claire' admits that she desires 'Madame,' and is teased and mocked for her impropriety and indiscretion. Gradually the game falls apart as the two bicker over what should come next in the narrative, and we realize that 'Madame' is actually Claire, and 'Claire' is actually Solange. We also discover that the sisters are actively conspiring against their employers and have already gotten rid of the man of the house referred to only as 'Monsieur,' who, like Snowball in *Deathwatch*, is discussed but never appears."

"Did they kill him?" Emily asked in rapt attention. She took another large swig of wine.

"No, they framed him for a crime via an anonymous letter to the police."

"Ah shucks."

"They are saving murder for Madame herself, whom they plan to poison. As the two sisters plot and scheme, they become ever more excited and delirious. They admit that they love each other, and are possibly *in love*, and despise each other in equal measure."

"I get that," Emily said with a pronounced nod of her head, her dark blue eyes aglow from the light of the fire. "That speaks to me."

"They also despise themselves," I said, "and yearn for a life with dignity. Madame, they feel, is the single obstacle in the way of their imagined better life. They are financially and emotionally oppressed by her, they lust for her, they are envious of her, and therefore, they loathe her. They gleefully conspire to poison her, then chop her into bits and bury her remains."

"That is marvelous!" she squealed.

"It is. However, as the plan reaches a fevered pitch, Madame comes home unexpectedly, taking the maids by surprise. Claire runs off to prepare the poisoned tea as Solange tends to Madame's various ever-shifting whims. It is here where we discover that, although Madame is manic, flighty, and self-absorbed, she is neither as cruel nor as erotically sadistic as Claire had portrayed her. Indeed, not only does Madame *not* sexually dominate her maids, she does not appear to acknowledge them as sexual beings at all. To her, they may as well be loyal dogs. Instead, in typical Genet fashion, Madame suddenly finds herself tremendously aroused by Monsieur *now that he is incarcerated*. Madame works herself into such a manic frenzy that she begins to give away her expensive finery to Claire and Solange, declaring that she only wants to make them happy, as they desperately try to get her to drink the poisoned tea. After hearing that Monsieur has been released on bail, Madame wants celebratory champagne instead of tea. She runs off to fuck his brains out, and she remains un-poisoned."

"Damn it!" Emily exclaimed.

"I know, it's a bummer," I said. "Despondent and broken, the maids resume their sadomasochistic role-playing game, though this time it is considerably more vicious and overtly sexual. Solange—playing either Claire or herself or an amalgam of both—grabs a riding whip from the wall and forces Claire-as-Madame onto her knees and makes her crawl on the ground like a wriggling worm."

"Mmmm…" Emily purred.

"Claire submits to the degradation at first, though it is unclear if she is a willing participant or is simply too afraid to resist. She finally begs Solange to stop, but Solange refuses to break character until Claire begins gagging, whimpering that she is going to be sick, and crawls away. And then they kill themselves, I think. I can't remember."

"I want to read that! Please grab it for me!"

I went into the cabin and retrieved my dog-eared copy of *The Maids* from my bookbag.

"It's worth noting," I said as I handed her the script, "that *The Maids* was not simply a product of Jean Genet's fevered imagination, but was inspired by the crime of the notorious Papin sisters. In 1933, while working as live-in maids for Monsieur René Lancelin, Christine and Léa Papin brutally murdered Lancelin's wife and adult daughter. What is curious is, for all of *The Maids'* supposed transgression… homosexual incest, sadomasochism, suicide, the glorification of crime and murder, and so on… the actual real-life inspiration for the play was a far more sordid and transgressive affair than the play itself. The Papin sisters, whom by all accounts were essentially kept as slaves in the Lancelin house and worked seven days a week with virtually no rest, succeeded in killing their Madame, unlike their fictional counterparts. And not only did they kill her, but they ripped out her eyeballs and bludgeoned her and her daughter with hammers and pewter pots until their heads were an unidentifiable goop."

"Oh my..." she gasped.

"Then they went upstairs and fucked like mad women."

Emily moaned and bit her lip. "Were they twins? Please tell me they were identical twins."

"Sisters yes, twins no. In Genet's play, it is strongly suggested that Claire and Solange are attracted to one another, but it's unclear if they ever fully act upon those impulses. The Papin sisters, however, actually had, in no uncertain terms, an active sexual relationship."

"Of course they did!" Emily exclaimed. "Wouldn't you?"

"Uh..."

"What other choice did they have?!"

"Okay, fair," I said. "And why Genet would be drawn to the Papin case is not difficult to see. The violence, the profane sexuality, the subversion of both accepted morality and oppressive power dynamics are all well within the Jean Genet wheelhouse. And yet, he passed on the opportunity to present these elements on stage in all of their blood-soaked glory. But why? Why not conclude his play with the sisters naked in bed together—as the Papin sisters were when the mutilated bodies of their victims were found—their hands still red with the blood of a fresh kill?"

Thank you for attending my lecture.

Emily shuddered. "Oh wow," she said, breathing heavily. "Now *that* is theatre."

"Yeah," I said. "Craig Lucas is good too, though."

After a while we simply sat in silence, settling deeply into the outdoor sofa, the fire crackling, Billie Holiday crooning on the stereo, watching the tree branches dance in the breeze. Emily put her knees under her chin, stretched her oversized sweater over her bare legs, and drifted off to sleep, wrapped in the down comforter from her brother's bed. I hadn't felt particularly tired, but I must have drifted off as well.

***

I was awakened by the vibrations of the couch. As my eyes slowly adjusted, I could see the silhouette of Emily reading Jean Genet by firelight, moaning and panting, the blanket flapping quicker and quicker.

I did not move or make a sound, but she must have sensed that I was awake because she said, "Don't look at me... I'm so close... I'm soooooo CLOSE..."

She all but screamed as she reached her climax, the couch rocking and wobbly on its short legs.

"Oh GOD...oh god..." she gasped. "I'm sorry... I c-couldn't... I couldn't help myself..."

"It's fine, Ms. Conlin."

"Please don't put this in the book."

"I won't."

She fell back asleep, still cooing and whimpering.

I must have cashed out again too. I don't remember any nightmares, queer or otherwise, but I am pretty sure that they happened.

When I awoke later, it was still pitch black out. I was alone on the sofa. The down comforter was draped over me.

"Emily?"

No answer.

I walked over and peeked my head in the door of the cabin.

"Em?" I called out. Nothing.

I ran to the edge of the deck and jumped down into the grass. As I started down the hill toward the lake, I saw Emily's scarf lying in the mud.

"What the fuck is going on here?!

I could hear a faint sound coming from the lake.

Singing.

As reached the retaining wall, I could tell that it was Emily. I could vaguely see her down below, sitting on the tiny boat dock, leaning over, peering directly into the still water.

"Emily, what are you doing?"

She didn't respond, just continued singing.

"*And when I grow too old to dream / I'll climb inside a hole and sleep…*"

"Emily! Don't move, I am coming down!"

"*And when I rise again it will be as something low…*"

I stepped carefully onto the dock.

"*Something slow / at the left hand of Lucifer…*"

"Do not move, Emily."

"I just wanted to dip my toes in the cool water," she said. She wasn't doing that, however. She continued to lean over the edge, staring straight into her own reflection in the lake's black mirror.

"Em," I said gently, but firm, "will you scooch back from the edge there, please? You are making me very nervous right about now."

"Sometimes I think about following her," she said quietly, continuing to stare at her reflection in the ripples. "All the way down." She seemed very drunk.

"I don't like that," I said. "Please move back."

"I thought you could swim. I thought you were here to save me."

"You were right to doubt me, Em. I'm a total fraud. Now please move back from the edge."

"I need to take you upstairs. We haven't done that yet."

"You're right. Let's do that. Let's do that now."

"Do you have your notebook with you?"

I tapped my jacket pocket. "I have this one," I said. "I keep a small spiral notebook and pen in this pocket at all times."

She nodded.

"Should we go upstairs, then? Now? To the circle room?"

"I can't wait."

She stood up, swaying softly, gliding her bare soles against the splintery, untreated wood planks. "That is where I saw her."

"Saw who?"

"There," she said, vaguely pointing into the dark of the night, "across the room, standing in the opposing doorway... There she was. It was her. It was me. She was me. Emily Conlin."

I finally coaxed her back up the hill to the deck. Outside Emily remained, refusing to go inside the cabin. I again insisted that she wrap the down comforter around herself.

"I can't do that," Emily mumbled, slurring her words a bit. "She isn't here."

There was a bit of wine left, and she proceeded to polish it off. I tossed some more ash logs on the smoldering fire and stoked it back to flame. I can't remember if there was still music playing or not. I never shut it off, but I do not remember any sound but silence, save the wind.

"The first night was rough," she said as we sat again on the outdoor sofa. "There was screaming all night. Emily and me, we found a small bedroom of our own, with a window looking out into the woods. Barricaded the door with a chest of drawers. Just as we were told to do. Sat on the bed and watched the doorknob rattle and twist. They knew we were new. They knew we were soft. They wanted in. We pressed our feet against the dresser and hoped we were strong enough. We cried. We wanted Mommy to hold us and make it all better. But she died while we were locked up inside." She began to cry.

"Take your time," I said, writing. "We are not in a rush."

"The first night stretched on for days and nights," she sniffled. "The days outside were bright and cheery, but we did not dare move the barricade. The nights were filled with screams, and bangs, and rattling doorknobs. At least we didn't kill each other like a lot of people do. Instead, we just made love all the time. And we became whomever we wanted to be. For ourselves... for each other... whomever we wanted. My favorite was Jason..."

"He had a name?" I asked, trying to write down everything she said.

"That's what we named him. He was better than every other man in the house. He was the best a man could ever possibly be. To our exact specifications."

"She was Jason? For you?"

"Until she decided not to be. That made me mad."

Outside Emily proceeded to tell me about all of the horrors and revelations of the house near Down Pattersons. The various people who arrived and then could not escape once they met their *other* ("only one comes in, only one can ever leave"); the depravity and violence, the boredom, the role-playing, the power-plays, the abuse and the tenderness, all within the conceit this was happening to both Emily and the *other Emily*, sometimes together, sometimes apart. She told me about the silent, shrouded woman who never uncovered her face, even in the midst of assault and/or ecstasy. Even when she was bound and beaten. She told me of the two overly macho men, identical in every way who, over time, evolved into completely different people—one flamboyant and fabulous, the other a snarling, feral beast so violent and out of control that he had to be chained up in his room or locked in the basement (still good for the occasionally screw, though). She talked of others. Many others. Many and few. Others who came but seldom went. Others who died horribly. Many others.

She told me of occasionally seeing her brother through a window, but never being able to get his attention. (Seth confirms frequently looking for Emily over the years, but claims to have never seen anything through the broken windows of the derelict and dilapidated house). Emily also told me of a tryst she ("and Emily") had with a minor, or possibly a pair of minors, that may have ended in tragedy. After some cajoling, the Burlington police department did admit to receiving an APB about a runaway from Southwest Kentucky. There has been no confirmation that he was ever spotted in the greater-Burlington area. Nevertheless, if the blood that Emily was covered in near Down Pattersons is a match to this boy's (boys'?), state PDs should likely be notified. That is none of my business, however.

Dawn broke as Emily finished her tale; her eyes glassy like dark blue marbles. She looked exhausted and lost. Her lips trembled. I picked up the blanket from the deck and draped it over her shoulders. She continued to shiver, swaying like the branches of the trees around the lake.

I tucked my small spiral notebook and pen back into my jacket pocket, exhaling deeply, not quite sure how, exactly, to proceed. I was fairly certain that Emily would not be pleased with the inevitable next phase of this project. My assumptions would prove accurate.

At the risk of playing armchair headshrinker, it seemed quite evident to me at the time that Emily showed clear signs of fantasy-prone personality disorder onset by severe trauma. And although I did not (nor do I currently) have access to a recent edition of the DSM [*and, as I'm sure you figured by now, my phone no longer works here*], I was then inclined to assume that the level of dissociative narcissism (narcissistic dissociation?) Emily exhibited may have been on the extreme end of the spectrum. But was not in any sense unheard of. It was curious what I took to be her fantastical confabulations neither elevated her nor particularly shifted blame upon the "other Emily." Indeed, it occasionally illustrated a tremendous amount of grief and remorse for what she considered to be her own transgressions. But again, this could likely have been explained by what appeared to be mental, psychological, and possibly even physical trauma she experienced over two full decades. It is not at all uncommon, of course, for victims of traumatic circumstances to self-blame. Though, within the narrative, it was never entirely clear to me who precisely were the victims and who were the abusers (at least with any consistency. Perhaps those roles within the environment were hazily defined and in flux). I found it particularly telling that she would frequently attempt to implicate me as a co-conspirator after-the-fact. ("Wouldn't you have done that?" she would say. "Wouldn't you have done the same?")

Unfortunately, clear and definitive details were thin on the ground when we reached the end of our conversation that frosty morning at Rock Lake.

"I like this story," I told her. "I like it a lot. But there are gaps. Gaps I don't think you're in any state to fill."

"What?! What are you talking about?"

"I think our story needs some... how should I put this... impartial field research."

Predictably enough, she did not take this well. She began screaming at me as I turned to walk into the cabin to gather my things.

"Are you joking?!?! Please tell me you are joking!!!"

As I passed through the kitchen toward the main room, I tapped the panic button on the underside of the counter.

"I am not joking."

"Please don't go into that house!" she cried. "You won't ever come out!"

"I need to see it for myself," I said as I threw my bags over my shoulder and moved toward the front door.

She walked toward me urgently, her hands folded in front of her.

"Please, please, I'll do better. I'll do a better job of being descriptive. I've just never done this before!"

"You did fine, Emily. There are just some things I need to check out to do the thing justice."

"You can't do this!"

"I'm just going as an observer, okay?"

"That's BULLSHIT!" she shrieked, tears streaming down her cheeks, her face as red as Seth's when he laughed. It was kind of adorable. "YOU'LL RUIN EVERYTHING!"

"I won't." I pulled out my phone and dialed 911. I told them I was leaving immediately, and she's not safe alone, so please hurry. I'm sure they heard her hysterics in the background, which hopefully lit a fire under their collective blue ass to get to the cabin with all due speed.

"Thank you very much for the gripping yarn, Emily," I said as I departed. "Please keep the Genet script. My gift to you. I'll see you again, some sunny day."

"I DOUBT IT!" she screeched as she shrank in my car's rearview mirror. "I'll never see YOU again!!!"

"I promise," I said to her diminishing reflection. "I promise."

I had no intention of lying. I promise.

The House Just North of Pattersons Creek

Seth and Emily were right; "Down Pattersons" is nothing much at all. I honestly don't think I could consider it a town. It is a smattering of houses, a restaurant tavern, a one-floor community center/library/church, and a single broken road. Even though, as far as I could tell, it is the closest central spot to the house where I could have parked, I would most certainly have gotten lost had I started there. Instead, I left my car on the berm of Route 50 and hiked into the forest.

Emily had undersold how burned out and desiccated the house was on the outside. It appeared as though the brambles and briars would overtake it within the decade, if that long. Walking the perimeter, one would reasonably assume that no one had stepped near the place in half a century or more, except that, on the back-left side. A basement window had been recently replaced with fresh safety glass (no vent shaft, though). The calking was still smooth. I kicked at the window with the heel of my left boot. *Sturdy enough.* I kicked it a few more times and managed to start a small crack in the thick, barely translucent glass. I kicked it a few more times, and the fissure grew a bit wider.

As I walked up the steps to the porch, I felt as though I might break the dry-rotted planks and fall right through. Alarm bells rang loudly in my head.
Hear the loud alarum bells—
Brazen bells!

119

What tale of terror, now, their turbulency tells…

…as Poe would say. In hindsight, I probably should not have ignored them. But I did, alas. *Alas.* So in I went.

The interior was nice enough, I suppose. Incongruently nice, given the outside of the place. Quaint, but drab. And drafty. A damp chill hung in the air. "Hello?" I shouted, but heard nothing in return save the faint buzzing in my ears, which I had brought in with me. I noticed a single pair of pine green flip-flops in the foyer that had clearly been kicked off haphazardly, but I could not determine how long they had been there. Very little dust on them. I also couldn't help but notice scratches and gouges in the frame around the door and on the hardwood floor below it. There was no mat or throw rug by the door, but there were dark discolorations in the wood. "Is anyone home?" I asked, a bit louder this time. Still no response. I wondered if I should take my boots off as the owner of the flip-flops had done, but I opted not to. *Just being cautious.* I did leave my bags there.

From the foyer, I entered what I took to be the parlor. Old, mauve, flower-print loveseat. Dusty coffee table. Full bookshelves which contained what appeared to be mostly outdated textbooks, cross-genre, multidisciplinary. Several I recognized and knew to contain incorrect or incomplete information. Bits of (deliberate) fiction were scattered about the shelves as well. There did not seem to be any particular rhyme or reason for how the books were arranged, except for one shelf which contained the Kurt Vonnegut collection in order of publication from *Player Piano* to *Galapagos*. Conspicuous by its absence was *Mother Night*. I went back to my duffle bag by the front door to retrieve the $2.75 paperback I had bought in Palo Alto and placed it on the shelf between *The Sirens of Titan* and *Cat's Cradle*.

On the top shelf of one of the cases, mixed in with a series of Mediterranean cookbooks, was a first-edition hardcover copy of my second novel. I nearly missed it, for the dust jacket was gone. Clearly Emily's assertion that the parlor bookshelves contained no blood and screwing had been slightly off base. I took it down from the shelf to give it a look. *To Cindy*, former me had written on the title page, *Keep Art Dangerous.*

"Jesus," I muttered to myself out loud, "how many copies did I sign for that broad?" I placed it back where I had found it, as no better location was evident.

Of particular interest to me was a 1920s-style Gramophone complete with tin horn by the doorway to the hall. Next to it was a small record shelf which contained exactly two LPs, both from 1957: Nat 'King' Cole's *After Midnight*, and *Body and Soul*, by Billie Holiday. I suppose I will never know why those were the only two albums in the house, but if just two were to be had, you could certainly do worse. I am particularly fond of the latter, even though it is a bit bluesier than I might typically prefer.

I walked down a short hallway to what appeared to be a living room, and it was there that I encountered the first signs of life in the house. Lying on her back across one of two couches was a young woman, a girl really, sixteen or seventeen I would guess, holding a small, round mirror above her face. She wore an oversized gray crew neck sweater, matching shorts, and a plastic beaded bracelet on her right ankle the same color as the flip-flops by the front door. Her left knee was up and bent, her right leg lay across it, her right knee skinned and raw, her right foot bouncing nervously. Her foot bounced faster and faster, her breathing grew ever more erratic, and I wondered if she might be having a panic-attack. Feeling like a creep standing there, I tried to think of the least-threatening way to make my presence known. Short on ideas, I went for the classic clearing-of-the-throat. She shot up quickly with a tiny squeal as she dropped the mirror to the floor and quickly brushed the jungle of dark ginger curls away from her face. She stared at me, panting and quivering, the whites of her eyes wide and round, jade irises surrounding dilated pupils. She grabbed a white wool scarf

121

from the headrest and held it to her chest as if I had intended to take it.

"Hi there," I said.

She sat cross-legged, still panting, looking furtively about. There was no one else around as far as I could tell.

"Hi there," she said, finally.

"How are you?" I asked.

"How are *you*?" she replied.

"Fine, thank you. May I sit?"

"Sit," she said, indicating space on the couch. I did, at the furthest-most spot. The walls of the room contained no art, only mounted mirrors in picture frames. The stone hearth fireplace looked to have been long cold, the bits of ash within it more likely from paper than from wood logs. On the hardwood floor in front of the fireplace were two large, dark stains, identical in size and shape.

"Quiet today?" I asked.

"Quiet today."

"Is it like this always?"

"Always."

"Figured." I indicated another doorway to the left. "That's the kitchen?" I asked.

"That's the kitchen," she confirmed with a nod. I got up and walked over to see for myself.

It was dark, lit only by a single candle on the marble counter, but I did see the large skylight overhead. Though the day was overcast, it was not at all difficult to imagine how oppressive the light would be in there on a sunny day.

There was another door leading off the living room. It was shut tight and, I assumed, locked. Beside it a key dangled from a hook on the wall.

"This is pretty much what I anticipated," I said, returning to the couch. "More or less. Although, I must say, I didn't expect you."

"I didn't expect *you*."

"Apologies," I said. "I didn't mean to interrupt." She shrugged.

"So...have you been here a long time?"

"Long time," she said.

"What's your name?"

"What's *your* name?"

"I see." Pause. "I guess Genet would just call you Green Eyes." She nodded. "This isn't bad. I maybe expected a little worse."

"Worse?"

"Like, more, like, ghostly, or ghoulish or some shit."

"Some shit."

"But that's all right. I can always spice it up a bit once the drafting starts. Really make it pop in revision. You know?"

"No."

"Lay on the drama. Give the people what they want. You know? Blood! Right? And screwing." She nodded. "I'm not just here for the facts; I'm here for the truth. okay? There's a difference, right?"

"Right," she replied.

"Between fact and truth?"

"Truth."

"There is a difference," I said. She shrugged again. She shrugged a lot. "I'll tell you the truth, little bean. If I'm the one bleeding words onto the page, it's *my* story. Do you feel me?"

"Feel me," she whispered.

"My words, my story. My lens. That's the truth." She nodded again.

We sat in silence for a bit. I heard neither creak nor peep from the rest of the house. "So..." I continued, "I hear that folks around these parts usually have an...*other*." She did not respond. Instead, she caressed her cheek with the white wool scarf. "So...?"

"So?"

"Where...is *your* other?" I asked.

"Other?"

"You have no other?"

"No other."

"So then…you're not trapped?"

"Trapped?!"

"I mean, you don't *have* to be here?"

"YOU don't have to be here!"

"I'm writing a book."

"That's not important."

"I'm getting paid to write a book."

"Fuck you!" Without warning, she lunged across the couch toward me, her lips aimed right for mine. *Whoa!* Instinctively, I recoiled from her. *Not today, shorty.* She returned to the other side of the couch looking quite stunned. "You think I'm ugly."

I tried not to laugh.

"No one would ever think you're ugly."

"*You're* ugly."

"That's not nice." *True enough, though.*

Again we sat in silence for a good while. Outside grew ever darker. A storm began to brew, and the windows rattled from the wind.

Finally, small and pouty, the girl said, "Emily kisses me."

Okay…here we go…

"I am sure she does."

"Sure she does."

"How long has it been since you last saw Emily?" The girl looked at me askance, as if she did not entirely understand my question. I tried a different word order. "Since you last saw Emily, has it been a long time?"

"A long time," she said with a nod.

"Where is Emily now?"

"Where is Emily now…In our bedroom."

"In this house?"

"In this house."

"Upstairs?"

"Upstairs."

Hmmmmm…

"Of course, she is. And why are you not up there with her?"

"She wanted to be with herself." Pause. "And I'm not Emily." Pause. "Yet."

"I don't recall hearing of you. You must be new."

"Must be new."

"And if you wanted to, you could just walk away."

"Walk away?"

"Couldn't you walk away?"

"WALK AWAY?!"

"This will get old quick."

I had not realized it at first, but at this point she was looking right over my shoulder, sour-faced and annoyed.

"*This* will get old quick." She craned her neck and shouted, "No one is impressed, you boring thing!"

I turned around and was startled to see a faceless figure standing in the doorway, half obscured by shadow.

"Oh fuck!" I exclaimed.

The figure's head was covered in what I could best describe as an opaque wedding veil, bobbing from side to side like blind musicians do.

"Ignore her," the girl said. "She just wants attention."

I stood up and turned toward the figure, retrieving my small notebook and pen from my jacket pocket.

"Good evening, ma'am," I said. "I am writing a piece on you all today. Is that okay with you?" The shrouded woman nodded but said nothing. "Could I ask you a few questions?" The shrouded woman nodded but said nothing. "Um... If I ask you questions, will you answer me?" The shrouded woman nodded but said nothing. "If I ask you questions, will you answer me with words that come out of your mouth so I can hear them?" The shrouded woman nodded but said nothing. "Wonderful. How long have you been a resident here?" The shrouded woman nodded but said nothing. "Would you say several years?" The shrouded woman nodded but said nothing. The girl on the couch covered her mouth, falling into a fit of giggles. "Decades?" The shrouded woman nodded but said nothing. "Tell me about the family you left behind." Nothing. "Tell me who is waiting for you on the outside." Nothing. "Do you think they miss you?" The shrouded woman shook her head and said nothing. She retreated into the dark of the hallway until I could no longer see her. "Thank you, ma'am. Most illuminating."

"Told ya to ignore her," the girl said, still giggling.

I stood dumb, looking at the empty doorway, wondering what to do next as the girl's tittering continued to mock me.

Suddenly, another figure appeared where the shrouded woman had been. Another woman. Mid-thirties for sure, smartly dressed in well-fitting designer jeans, a black halter top which matched her pristine manicure and pedicure. Her dark hair lay in a perfect, straight bob, her make-up flawless, as if she had just come fresh from the salon. *But, of course, that's impossible...right?*

Her demeanor was confident, almost *swaggery*. She was flushed, and slightly out of breath. She sized me up before taking a seat on the couch next to the girl, who beamed at the sight of her, cuddling close and resting her head on the woman's shoulder. I resumed my place at the other end of the couch.

"Who is this, baby?" the woman asked, twisting the girl's hair around her index finger. "A new friend?"

"A new friend."

"Hello, new friend."

I should have been prepared for this, but I was not.

"Hello. Hello, Ms. Conlin."

"So formal," Emily said.

"Formal," the girl echoed.

"Sweet baby, have you been courteous to our guest?"

"He thinks I'm ugly."

"Of course I do not." Pause. "It is... it's good to see you, Emily."

She looked at me with a raised eyebrow. "Have we met?"

"You could say."

Emily's face darkened, but then she smiled.

"How wonderful for you."

"Wonderful," the girl said.

"Do you have news for me then?"

"That is not why I'm here," I replied.

"Well, that's a shame."

"Shame," said the girl.

"I needed a broader perspective," I told them. I held up my notebook and pen.

"Broader perspective?" the girl asked.

"Well, broaden away," Emily said. "Our services, such as they are, are at your disposal."

"Much obliged," I said.

"We'll see." She shouted toward the doorway, "Get our guest some tea and biscuits, boring thing!" I heard shuffling out in the hallway that grew distant. *There must be another door to the kitchen,* I thought. "Have you had a chance to poke around?" she continued.

"He thinks I'm ugly," the girl said.

"No, I don't," I said. "But no, just this story so far. And not even all of it."

"Well, be careful. It can be treacherous. And we want you to write nice things about us."

"Nice things."

"Little girl," I said, "why haven't you been up to the circle room yet?"

"I don't want two of me," the girl said dreamily, intertwining her fingers with Emily's. I noticed Emily had a thin gold bracelet on her right wrist, and a matching one on her ankle. If not actual gold, they were very authentic-looking fakes. "I want more of her."

"Isn't she just the sweetest?" Emily said, her eyes twinkling midnight blue.

"Is that an option, Emily? Is it possible? What if you went back in?"

"Do you think I haven't?" she replied, a knit in her brow

telling me precisely how stupid I was for even asking. "Do you really think I haven't tried?"

"Just curious."

"Curious," the girl said.

"Oh, curious, curious boy… just the one. That is all you get. It's a pity."

"It IS a pity," the girl said.

"I hope you don't get cold feet, new friend."

"Cold feet," the girl said.

"Do you have cold feet? You do strike me as the curious type."

"All in good time," I replied.

"Good time," the girl said with a nod.

The shrouded woman entered from the kitchen struggling to carry a tray of biscuits and cups. I hadn't noticed it before, but her left hand was bandaged into a ball. There was blood on the bandages. I stood to help, but Emily waved her hand for me to sit down. The shrouded woman set the tray on the other couch, then went back into the kitchen. The girl giggled, and Emily shushed her, grinning. A moment later the woman returned awkwardly carrying the small, dusty coffee table from the parlor. At this point I could not bear to remain ungentlemanly any longer and stood to take the table from her. It was surprisingly thick and heavy. Emily "hmph'd" in mild disappointment. I set the coffee table on the floor between the two couches, and the shrouded woman placed the tray clumsily upon it, cups and saucers rattling. She picked the small mirror off the floor and laid it on the coffee table as well.

From the kitchen came another lady, late-sixties/early seventies I would wager, carrying a carafe of tea. She smiled at me, polite but strained, and set the carafe next to the biscuits and cups. Also on the tea tray were two serrated knives.

"Well now," the lady said, taking a seat next to the shrouded woman on the other couch. "Isn't this just a pretty bit of business here."

"What happened to her hand?" I asked. The shrouded woman covered her bandaged hand with her sleeve.

"It doesn't matter anymore," the other lady replied.

"Doesn't matter anymore," the girl agreed.

"Can't you show her any sympathy?" I asked.

"Sympathy is pity," the girl said, "and pity is pitiful."

"I think you're just repeating words you don't mean," I said.

"Mean!"

"Angel, be calm," Emily said to the girl. She turned toward the other couch. "That is quite enough for you, boring thing."

The shrouded woman bobbed her head back and forth. Emily and the older lady looked right at each other. I got the sense that there was a silent power play at work. After a moment or two, the older lady smiled and nodded.

"Why don't you go rest a bit, darling," she said to the shrouded woman, patting her gently on the arm. The shrouded woman stood and shuffled out to the hallway. I heard steps creaking.

The older lady smiled pleasantly at me but did not speak, the left sole of her white sensible shoe tapping softly on the hardwood floor. She brushed a strand of winter white hair from her face. Emily and the girl cuddled and kissed, whispering and giggling to one another, seemingly unperturbed by my presence on the opposing end of the couch. Emily wrapped the wool scarf loosely about the girl's neck. I poured tea from the carafe into the four ceramic cups, which steamed and bubbled.

"So..." I said finally, "what would you good folks be up to if I were not here?"

"Why, waiting for you, honey pie," the older lady said. She made no move to pick up a cup of tea. "Of course."

"Of course," the girl said.

"You are curious about the house, I'm sure," the older lady said.

"A bit," I replied. I indicated the two large stains in the wood in front of the fireplace. "I'll bet there's a story here, yes?"

"Not really," Emily said. "Nothing to write about."

"An old house like this," the older lady said, "messes do happen."

I considered writing "messes do happen" in my notebook, but I figured I would remember it.

"Fair enough," I said.

"Would you like a tour, dear?"

"Possibly," I replied. "That might be nice. I like your parlor, though I must say I am a bit underwhelmed by your music collection. And the selection of books, for that matter."

"No blood, right?" the girl said, echoing me from before. "And screwing."

"Well, there is some," I admitted, "but that's true. Mostly outdated texts. Very little of what we might call, as she said, blood and screwing."

The woman leaned toward me, smiling like the cover model of a lifestyles magazine for seniors. "Would you like to screw, dear?"

"All in good time," I said. *All in good time.* "I have heard of this place."

"What do you know?" Emily asked.

"DO you know?" asked the girl.

"Please," said Emily, "have a biscuit. You must have had quite a hike today."

I picked up a serrated knife from the tray, cut the biscuit in half and took a bite, skipping the marmalade.

"How does it taste?" the lady asked.

Okay, I thought, *Kinda yeasty.*

"Quite good," I said. "Thank you."

I picked up a cup of tea. The girl sat up and did as well.

"Careful, it's hot," Emily said. I put it to my lips, and the pain was immediate. I winced. It was nearly boiling. "I told you."

The girl took a hearty sip of hers and did not wince in the slightest.

"Something funny I noticed about your windows," I said.

"None of them are broken."

"What should you expect?" the lady asked.

"Wall-mounted mirrors in picture frames," I observed. "No pictures, ever. Just mirrors."

"Just mirrors," the girl said.

"I have not seen them yet, but I hear that there are two dining rooms: one upstairs and one downstairs. Identical in every way."

"In every way."

"Oak tables," I continued, looking over my notes, "hand-stitched linens, seats exactly seven."

"Only odd numbers," the older lady confirmed.

"Only ever odd numbers in the dining rooms," Emily said. "Somebody's idea of a joke. Rather cruel, really."

"Rather cruel," the girl confirmed.

"Hush now, sweet baby."

"Well," I said, "if I'm missing something here, I apologize for being dim, but that sounds like a pretty easy fix to me." Pause. "The sets are identical, right? So just carry a chair from one dining room to the next if you need to accommodate an even number of people." The three of them looked at me intently, but no one answered. The older lady ceased tapping her foot on the floor. "You know... up the stairs, down the stairs, not too difficult." Nothing. "I mean... I could do it for you if you would like."

"Well," the older lady said, "then they would no longer match, dear."

Pause.

Fair enough.

"And how about the cellar?" I asked, indicating the closed door. "I am definitely curious about the cellar."

"There is a fruit cellar," she said. "Fresh pickings. Quite delicious."

"How about the cold storage in the back?"

"Not quite as delicious."

"There's nothing for you there," Emily said.

"What about for you, Emily?" I asked.

"I don't go there. The smell does not suit me."

"Are there others about? I might like to meet them."

"They're here and there," Emily said. "The Dog is in the cellar. You would do well to avoid him."

"Avoid him," the girl agreed emphatically.

"How about a fellow named Jason? I've heard great things about him. I would really like to get to know him better."

Emily glowered at me, then attempted to mask what was clearly anger with a thin smile. It was not a success.

"Jason doesn't live here anymore," she said tersely. "He's gone, and he is never coming back." She looked away. "You're not his type, anyway."

"That is a shame," I said with a shrug.

"Shame, shame, shame," the girl said.

"Dearest," the older lady said to Emily, "you're not cross with our new friend, are you?"

"I am perfectly calm."

At once, we heard music from the other side of the hall—"Comes Love" from *Body and Soul*. Someone had put side B on the phonograph. We heard the ever-growing sound of wingtips tapping along the wood floors down the hall, and a voice singing along:

"Comes measles you can quarantine a room / comes a mousie you can chase it with a broom / comes love, nothing can be done…"

"He loves this song," the older lady said, though I am not sure to whom.

"Seriously, you guys," a man's voice said, growing closer, "why don't we just bring the record player in here?" He sauntered in, swigging from a bottle of *Chateau le Thys*. "We never hang out in the par—… Well, hello there," he said when he saw me.

Ballpark: late-forties, maybe fifty. Lean, muscular build, thick black hair just starting to gray at the temples, well-dressed but disheveled, in a black suit with white pressed shirt unbuttoned to the chest, as if he had just come from a fancy party that had gotten out of hand. His shoes had been recently polished and shined, but nonetheless looked scuffed beyond repair.

"Hello," I replied.

"Sorry, I have to finish this," he said, then proceeded to sing the rest of the song in a not-half-bad Billie Holiday impersonation, "*Comes a nightmare, you can always stay awake / Comes depression you may get another break / Comes love, nothing can be doooone…*"

He took a drink from the wine bottle and offered it to me.

"Good with tea, thanks," I said, holding up my cup. I had yet to swallow a sip. The girl finished her tea and poured another cup. The man arched his eyebrows and shrugged. He offered the bottle around the room. The girl took a swig, then handed it back to him. He plopped down on the sofa next to the older lady.

"So…you're new," he said to me with a sweeping point of his finger.

"Thus far."

"Dibs!" he shouted, putting up his hand.

"New friend," Emily said firmly. "Show some manners."

The man rolled his eyes and took another drink. "Psh. You used to be fun, Emily."

"No, I didn't."

"Have you had the grand tour, new friend?" the man asked with a big smile. He had very pretty teeth. "Would you like to go upstairs?"

"Perhaps," I said. "In a bit."

"Would you like to fuck?"

"Manners," Emily said, pointing a stern finger at him.

"All in good time," I replied.

"He said the exact same thing to me the first day we met," Emily told me.

I know, I thought.

"You sure that was me?" the man said with a shrug. "I'm

not so sure. It was a lifetime ago."

I blew on my tea and took a sip. It was sweetened with what tasted like raw sugar, balanced with lemon. There was also a sharply bitter undertone to the flavor that struck me as very familiar, but I could not quite place what it was, or how I recognized it. I took another sip. *Still not sure...*

"Your body is currency here," the man said. "That is all I'm saying."

"Manners!"

"The Dog would just love you—"

"MANNERS!"

"—into bloody little pieces."

"Little pieces," the girl said.

"Shut it, gash," the man said.

The man, the older lady, and Emily all laughed. The girl pouted.

"The Dog is your other, I'm assuming?" I asked him.

"The Dog would never bite me."

"Unless you beg him too," Emily said. They all laughed. *Hilarious.*

"The Dog made the little slit scream until she fainted," said the man.

"It doesn't matter," the girl said, irritated, her arms crossed. "The Dog bores me now."

"And yet, you keep going down there to give him treats."

The girl leapt up and shrieked, "I'LL EAT YOUR HEART!!!"

The man cackled and slapped his leg. He took another glug of wine and offered it to her. She drank, still frowning, and handed the bottle back to him.

"Sit, please, sweet angel," Emily said. The girl sat back down.

Gold, I thought, and wrote this all down in my notebook.

"What is this then?"

"He's a professional," the older lady said to the man.

"So you're on assignment?" he asked me.

"Impartial field research."

"One guess as to who sent him."

The man smiled at Emily; she scowled at him.

"She wouldn't," Emily said.

"She wouldn't?" the girl asked. "She who?"

"Hush now."

"You do have news then," the older lady said. "How is Kurtis?"

"Good old Kurtis," the man said, hoisting his bottle in salute. "He was a fun lay."

"He was," the older lady agreed with a pleasant smile. "Liked it rough."

"He blew off the top of his head with a shotgun," I told them.

They both howled with laughter.

"It is very sad," Emily said.

"Very sad," the girl agreed caressing Emily's arm.

"Poor Benny."

The older lady and the man laughed even harder.

"Your pain is delightful!" the man announced.

The girl grabbed a knife from the tray and jumped up again.

"I WILL HACK YOUR FUCKING GUTS OUT!!!"

"Sit, baby. Please."

The girl did, still seething. She put the knife back down.

"Pure fucking gold," I said aloud, writing. *This goddamn thing writes itself.* I took another drink of sweet/sour/bitter tea. The girl did as well.

"So how is she then?" the man asked me. "Tell us everything, and don't you spare a single drop of blood. You're screwing her, right?"

"Screwing her right," the girl said.

"I am not."

"Why not?" he asked, his hand on his chest in *faux*-surprise. "It is soooo easy! She barely even fights. You know she likes the dark things deep down."

"Stop now," Emily said.

"You know that."

"STOP. NOW."

"I only know what I know so far," I said. "I don't know enough."

"Enough," said the girl.

"Be honest," the man said, clearly enjoying getting under Emily's skin. "Is she like Kurtis now?"

"Stop it!"

"STOP IT!" the girl shouted.

"Is she dead?" he asked me.

"If she's dead I don't want to know!" Emily said, quaking with panic and anger.

"Did you kill her?"

"I DON'T WANT TO KNOW!" Emily screamed.

The girl flapped her hands nervously. She stared daggers at the man on the other couch. He grinned back. I really liked his smile, shit-eating though it was.

"She is not dead," I said matter-of-fact. Everyone seemed to calm down.

"Ah," the man said. "Well...good for her."

"Emily?" the girl said, light dawning in her jade-green eyes. She looked at me and pointed vaguely toward the nearest window. "You're talking about Emily? You know Emily out there?"

"Sweet baby," Emily said, shooting me the *play along* look, "there is no Emily out there. Our new friend is just trying to be sensational."

"Yes," I affirmed. "Exactly that."

"Have some more tea, darling."

Emily poured the girl another cup. She drank. I finished mine, and it was at that point when I noticed that only the girl and I were drinking tea. I put my empty cup down. The aftertaste, bitter and maddeningly familiar, lingered.

"How many others are here?" I asked.

"Many and few," the older lady said.

"We could introduce you," the man said to me. "One by

one. Two by two. Oops, sorry Emily."

"Go fuck yourself," she said.

"Fuck yourself," the girl echoed.

"I am sure that he's sleeping right now," the man said with a smirk. "But, as our new friend here says, all in good time."

"There is time yet," the older lady said. "There is always time."

"Time enough," Emily agreed.

"Time enough…" the girl yawned. She set her cup down, appearing to be drifting into a stupor.

"Oh, it is so late!" Emily said.

"So late…" the girl slurred.

It can't be that late, I thought, though it was completely dark out. The wind rattled the windows, and rain began to fall.

"I think my sweet girl is worn out."

"Worn out…" The girl leaned into Emily's arms and fell asleep, her head resting on Emily's shoulder. Emily wrapped her arms around her.

"And spent," Emily said, stroking the sleeping girl's hair. She cuddled her for a few moments, whisper-singing a lullaby in D#. At a certain point, she looked over to the man. "Would you carry my angel upstairs? Please?"

"*Avec plaisir.*"

He stood, polished off his wine, set the empty bottle on the coffee table, then scooped the girl into his arms. The white wool scarf fell from her neck to the floor. Emily picked it up and draped it across the armrest of her side of the couch.

"To MY room," Emily said. "No others."

"What about—"

"No. Not ever."

"I could take her downstairs," he said. "She likes it down there."

"Upstairs. To my room."

"You used to be fun, Emily."

"That is simply not true."

"Good evening to you, handsome stranger," the man said to me, bowing his head in salute. *Hilarious.* "I shall see you in my dreams."

"Not if I see you first," I replied. "I must say, you really do remind me of Billie. It is rather uncanny."

The blood drained from the man's face, his arrogant flare fading before me. His eyes grew wide, and the corners of his lips curved down.

"Why..." he whispered, "why would you say that to me?"

"Your voice," I said. "Your Billie Holiday impression. It is eerily spot on."

"Oh," he replied, distant and small, nodding softly. "Appreciate it."

The man exited to the hallway not quite as jauntily as when he had entered, carrying the girl, limp in his arms. Creaking on the stairs. Without a word, the older lady gathered the uneaten biscuits and marmalade, the mirror, the bottle, and all but my teacup onto the tray. She also left the carafe and both serrated knives. She smiled and nodded to Emily and me, then exited into the kitchen.

We were alone.

We did not speak.

We listened to the rain.

I set my spiral notebook down on the table and put my pen in my jacket pocket.

"It is curious," she said finally.

"Is it?"

"You feel that you have spent time with me before. But I've never met you until now."

"That is precisely how I feel whenever someone reads me."

"But that's different. That is just a constructed version of you. And not an honest one."

"You echo me."

"Fair enough."

"How are you getting on?"

"There is a certain serenity in hopelessness."

"That's not something you would want to get used to."

"You would be amazed what you can get used to."

"Regrets then?"

"There was never any doubt in my mind that I would come in here some day."

"Some sunny day."

"It was never a question of if."

"Just when."

"And six days after my fifteenth birthday seemed like as good a time as any." Pause. "Seth and I were out walking in the woods..."

"Mushroom hunting?" I asked, though it wasn't really a question.

"Yeah..." she replied. I could tell that she had not given the specific details much thought in a while. "We were out looking for mushrooms, and we just so happened to come across the house."

"'*C'mon, Em, quit yer foolin' around*,'" I said, doing my best Seth impression. It is a work in progress.

"I miss him," she said.

"I'm sure."

"I miss my mom. I miss a lot of things."

I cannot relate, I thought.

"Of course," I said.

"I miss the touch of wind. The sting. I miss the morning dew. I miss the creek and the lake in the summertime, even though I can't swim. I miss the first snow of winter. I miss music. *Other* music. I miss the feel of grass under my feet."

She glided her bare soles softly across the hardwood floor.

"You remember the day?"

"Porch floorboards creaked..." she said absently. "For one split second, I thought twice about opening the front door, and just turning tail and running, but I'm a curious girl. I'm Emily Conlin."

"Always have been."

"Not always." Pause. "And so I stepped inside."

"Did you know yourself then?"

"I should hope so."

"Wonderful."

"I… I respect the house."

"Of course you do."

"Should we go upstairs?" she asked.

"Upstairs?"

"You and me? Now? To the circle room?"

"It can wait."

"We have always called it the circle room. But the room itself is not a circle at all. It's a perfect square. Total symmetry. Two identical red, crushed velvet divans." Pause. "Across the room, standing in the opposing doorway, there she was. It was her. It was me. She was me. Emily Conlin." Pause. "We were, for the moment, indistinguishable. We are the same girl."

"Still, you think?"

"I don't know. I don't know which one I was. I don't know which one I am." Pause. "She's… pretty?"

"Sure."

"But not as pretty as I wish she was. We like to think we look as nice as our last, best photo. But she didn't. So, of course, we didn't."

"One of you finally spoke."

"I was just about to say, Let's leave, and she said, 'Let's leave.' And in that moment, we were suddenly, slightly different people."

"She was slightly faster."

"By chance. You know, chaos. And chance. You should write that down."

"Nah."

"You could take off your jacket. You could stay."

"I could leave and come back."

"I don't think you can. I don't think it works that way."

"I could try."

"Are you boasting?"

I removed my jacket and tossed it onto the other couch. Emily poured me another cup of tea. I could still taste the lingering bitterness of my last cup, but I took a sip.

"Much obliged."

"We'll see," she said. "So... whose story is this? Emily's? Mine? Yours?"

"It's a story for everyone. It is the only story ever told. It's a story about a cage, and the people who love it."

"It is sad about Kurtis."

"You already knew about Kurtis, though. And yet, after all this time, you never told them."

"It's too sad."

"Is it?"

"I think it's sad."

"Do you? Or do you *think* you should?"

"I think I should."

"Kurtis thought he wanted out," I said. "But, of course, he didn't. No one wants out once they are. That's why his head exploded."

"Don't be silly. Kurtis is downstairs with his skull caved in. A pipe wrench, if I'm not mistaken."

"That explains quite a bit."

"Does it?"

"No."

"No, it doesn't."

"I thought there was serenity in despair."

"I said *hopelessness*."

"Ah, yes."

"Hopelessness and despair are two very different things. Right?"

"As different as fact and truth."

"Fact and truth are identical."

"You need to let her go, Emily."

"What are you talking about? *She* left *me*!"

"No, I mean the little girl upstairs. Let her go before she be-comes you."

"You can't take her from me."

"You are right about that. I can't. I'm just writing a book."

"That's not important."

"I'm getting paid to write a book."

"Fuck you! You can't take her from me; she IS me."

"Not yet she isn't."

"Close enough. Don't fancy yourself a liberator, new friend."

I lifted the cup to my lips for another sip of tea.

Instant regret.

My face felt hot and prickly. My stomach churned, and I felt dizzy and nauseated. I tried to tell her I thought I might be sick.

"I... I..."

But the words did not come.

"The facts won't set you free," she said.

I looked at my left hand. Shaking. Double vision.

"Truth... will..."

"It will," she said, inspecting my teacup. "You are correct about that."

And in that moment, I realized what that bitter flavor was.

"You'll pay..." I slurred, angry at her, but more at myself for being so foolish and careless. "Crush you..."

"That took longer than it should have," she said, setting the cup down.

"You'll suffer..." I growled through my teeth, black balloons popping in my eyes. I struggled to maintain.

"But you are bigger than she is."

"You... fuck..."

"All in good time."

I leaned back on the couch, still conscious, but feeling like a thousand-pound sack of gravel covered in wet gauze. Through the slits of my eyelids, I saw Emily stand and pick up my note-book from the coffee table. I struggled to breathe. She flipped through a few pages, looking for a moment like she may cry. Her face contorted briefly into anger, then she smiled. She saun-tered over to the door to the cellar, unlocked the door, and hung the key back on its hook. She opened the door and tossed my notebook down the stairs. "It's a treat, boy!" she said into the gaping chasm of black. "Get the treat!" She walked over to the other couch, leaving the cellar door wide open, and picked up my jacket. I might have been able to move if I really strug-gled, but it simply did not seem to be worth the effort. The little I could see through ever-dimming eyes was blurry and doubled. She draped the jacket over me like a blanket, bent down and kissed me on the lips. "Goodnight, Mr. Writer. Dream good things about us." She placed her index and middle fingers on my eyelids, shutting them.

Then dark.

THE DUPLICATION HOUSE: CELLAR

Chaos and Chance

Seth and Emily were right; "Down Pattersons" is nothing much at all. I do not honestly think I could consider it a town in any meaningful way. It's a smattering of houses, a one-floor church/library/community center, a restaurant bar, and a single, broken road. The forest abutted and surrounded the area on the northwest side. Pattersons Creek was in there somewhere, but I knew that just following it would not take me to the house.

Now what?

Unsure of what to do, I wandered around the area, tipping an invisible hat to the handful of people I saw. They nodded in reply.

I stepped into the only bar in town, a place called Kyles (no apostrophe). A sign by the door said THE KITCHEN IS OP N. *Something may be missing.*

A tiny brass bell jingled as I walked in. The place had the feel and appearance of a small, drafty barn, but it was oddly inviting all the same. A fire burned in the fireplace, and the three patrons at the time all sat at tables nearest the stone hearth. An older couple came in behind me, edging past with a "Beg pardon." I took a seat at the bar, and the fellow tending gave the older couple a "Hey y'all."

"Afternoon, Benji," they said in unison, and took a table near the fire.

He was probably my age, or thereabouts, with broad shoulders and a bit of a gut. He wore a Peterbilt cap and a thick, blue flannel shirt. "What can I gitcha, friend?" he asked me. "Menu?"

"Jack on the rocks," I said. "And sure." He handed me the paper menu. It was a lot of very deep-fried thisandthat, plus *Kyles* [sic] *Famous Minestrone*.

"How famous?" I asked.

"World famous," he deadpanned, placing my drink in front of me. "Anything grabbing ya?"

"I think I'll probably just stick to the whiskey," I said. "Doctor's orders."

"Good doctor."

He said hello to a few more folks walking in and handed them bottles of beer.

"You're not Kyle I take it?"

"Naw, Kyle was my uncle. He inherited the place from his pops when he passed. Shoulda been his brother Kurt's, rightly, but he passed a long time ago. Now they are all gone. Just tryin' to keep it in the family, you understand."

"Absolutely. You wouldn't happen to be Benjamin Haines, would you?"

He looked at me askance. "I might happen to be," he said, pouring hot coffees and two bowls of soup for the older couple that came in after me. He placed them on a tray and walked them over to the couple, continuing to talk to me. "Who's askin'? Here ya go, folks. Enjoy." He walked back to the bar.

"I am a friend of Seth Conlin's," I said. "You know, the landscaping guy?"

"Why would Seth Conlin be talking about me? He ain't lived here in a coon's age. Mr. Big-Time, you know?"

"Oh, he was just telling me once that he knew every single person in Down Pattersons. He mentioned you, among others. 'Good ol' Benny' he said."

"Ha," the man scoffed. "I ain't been called Benny since junior high. Even Seth should know that."

The door jingled, and a burly fellow in a leather coat and overalls led an elderly woman gingerly by the arm. The woman murmured to herself.

"Howdy, y'all," Benjamin said.

"Usual, Benj," the burly man replied, leading the woman to a table further back from the rest. Even from over in the corner I could still vaguely hear her muttering, for the joint was not large, and there was no television or music playing. Just the soft hum of quiet chatter. It was kind of maddening.

Benjamin continued pouring drinks and soups. He called back an order for a hamburger, but got no reply from the kitchen.

"Goddamn it," he sighed. "Guess I'm on grill too."

"What I am really searching for," I said to Benjamin, "is a house." He looked at me without so much as a flicker of recognition as to what I might be talking about. "To rent, I mean," I said, trying quickly to recover. "Or to buy."

"Well, we don't rent houses around here," he said, topping off my tumbler with Jack Daniel's. "As for real estate, you would need to drive over to Burlington proper to have that conversation. I don't know of nobody selling right now, though."

"Okay," I said. "I'm just trying to get out of the city, you know? I'm a writer by trade, and it is just too hectic out there. I need some woods and some babbling brook, *et cetera*. Seth told me that, for peace and quiet, Down Pattersons cannot be beat."

"Well, Seth was sure right about that," he chuckled, pouring two bowls of minestrone. "We sure got plenty of them." Pause. "He tell you bout his sister?"

I feigned surprise. "Didn't even know he had a sister."

"Shit," Benjamin said, wiping his hands on a small towel. "I prolly shouldn't have said nothing. I don't blame him for keeping her a secret. Chick is *messed up*."

"I won't tell," I said.

"Hey Tom!" Benjamin yelled over to the corner table, indicating the freshly poured bowls on a tray. "These are for you and B! Can you jump up and grab 'em? I gotta hop on back for a few."

"No problem," the burly man replied. Benjamin headed into the kitchen. I could still faintly hear the old woman murmuring in the corner, though the closer I listened the more her murmuring sounded like singing.

The muffled sound of the main guitar riff from "Don't Stop Believing" cut through the wash of subdued chatter. It was Tom's ringtone.

"Dang it all," the burly man said. "Gotta take this. I'll be right back, Auntie." He stood and walked toward the back door, the phone to his face. "Yeah?! What?" He exited, and I could see him through the windows pacing about near the picnic tables outside.

I returned to my drink, the bowls of minestrone soup steaming next to me. The aroma was rather enticing, as all I had eaten that day were some fortune cookies that were stuffed in my jacket. The closer I listened to the old woman, the more I recognized the song that she was singing ever so faintly to herself.

"*Soooooo…kissss meee…my sweet,*" she sang, "*and soooo let us part…*"

Well I'll be damned…

"*And when… I grow… too old to dream… your love… will live… in my heart…*"

I peeked through the divider to the kitchen and saw Benjamin sweating over the grill. Tom continued to pace and rant outside. I grabbed the tray of soup and walked it over to the corner where the old woman sat rocking back and forth and singing quietly to herself. I placed the soup in front of her and sat down. Her eyes were closed, and she continued to sing and rock, ignoring the soup. She did not appear to notice me at all.

"Ma'am," I whispered, "may I speak with you a moment?"

She did not acknowledge me.

"*After you've gone… life will go on…*" she sang.

"Ma'am?"

"*Like an old song we have sung…*"

"Did you use to work at the library, ma'am? Long ago?"

"Library…" she muttered, her eyes opening just slightly. She continued to hum the melody. "*Your love… will live…*"

"Ma'am, did your son go missing many years ago?" She

hummed a bit louder, her rocking intensified.

"*In my heaaaart...*"

"Did you go looking for him?" More rocking, more humming. "Did you go into a house looking for him? A house deep in the woods?" Tears began to gather in her barely opened eyes. "What was your son's name?"

"Doesn' matterrrr anymorrrre..." she said, humming and shaking.

Jackpot!

What was that word for a beneficial happenstance? I seem to have forgotten it somehow.

"Ma'am," I whispered urgently, "did you see him?"

She began crying and shaking her head. "They did thingsss..."

"Did you see your son in there?"

She shook her head vigorously, sobbing. "They did things to me in therrrre..."

"When you went in the house, did you see your son?"

"Grabbing and tearing at me..." she sobbed. "Chains...cellar..."

"Did you ever go upstairs?"

"Nooooo..." she cried. "Just the cellarrr... Heavy steel chainssss... tie you down... cold and hurt... they locked me... they did things... in pairs... in twos... they did things..."

"Did you see your son?!"

"Noooo...noooo...Hmmmm..."

"You just knew? You knew he was in there somewhere?"

"I know he waassss therrrre... didn't see him... but I knooooow..."

I started to get nervous as I felt eyeballs from every angle. I could see Tom through the window, still pacing outside on the phone. I held her hand, frail and bony. Her skin was loose and tissue-paper thin. Her wrist was scarred. Her other wrist was too.

"I want to help, ma'am," I said in a soothing whisper. "I am going to help. I promise."

"Kurt saw!" she sobbed, shaking her head, tears spilling down the deep creases in her face. "Kurtis watched them do things to me! Hurt me so bad! I begged help me! Two of them! Both of them! Just watched! Had to claw my way out the door!"

"I am going in, ma'am," I whispered. "But I need to know the way to the house."

She heaved in deep sobs, squeezing my hand as tightly as she could, which was not very tight at all.

"North... west... up the creek... then east..." she said. I could not quite follow, but I tried to retain it all. She continued squeezing my hand. "Through the briars, beyond the thicket, far from the hill..."

"What hill, ma'am? Which hill is it?"

"The fuck is this?!" a man shouted. It was burly Tom. "Who in hell are you?!"

I looked up at him. He was seething. His aunt continued to grip my hand and rattle off what I took to be directions. "Squeeze through...stand of Siberian larch..."

"Listen, Tom," I said, "lemme be straight with you right now. I am writing a book about the history of Down Pattersons. Your aunt is the only certified librarian in the town's history. I need to talk to her about what she knew. I didn't mean any harm here."

"History?!" he yelled. "Down Pattersons ain't got no history! Down Pattersons ain't even got a name."

"We were just talking," I said. The old lady nodded and sniffled, continuing to hold my hand.

"She don't talk," he growled. "She sings and she mutters. That's all she done for thirty-four years."

"That is just not true," I said. "When was the last time you actually tried to talk with her?" He grabbed me by the collar of my jacket and lifted me up, shoving his face right up to mine. *The scent of Kodiak Wintergreen is strong with this one.*

"Just let him go, Tommy," I heard Benjamin say. All eyes were on us now. He let go of my collar.

"You ain't got to talk to this shitheel tourist, Aunt Billie," burly Tom said. I backed away toward the door, dropping a $20 on the bar along the way.

"Bring him home!" Aunt Billie cried out to me as I backed out the front door. "Bring my baby home to me!!!"

Rather than leave my car in town, I opted to ditch it on the berm of Route 50.

Into the woods I went. *East from the creek...then north...through the briars, beyond the thicket, far from the hill...far from* what *hill...Is it a difficult one?*

I hiked for hours, it seemed, not really sure if I was heading in the proper direction. '*Midway upon the journey of our life,*' I thought, '*I found myself within a forest dark, for the straightforward pathway had been lost.*'

It grew darker at midday, and I could see storm clouds above. Hawks circled overhead. I saw a turkey buzzard. Then another. And then another. '*Ah me! How hard a thing it is to say what was this forest savage, rough, and stern, which in the very thought renews the fear.*' But which poet could lead me through this dark forest? *Whatcha got, West Virginia? Anybody have Marc Harshman's number?*

As the sky grew darker still, my olfactory senses were attacked by a coppery, septic blood stench. The more I struggled through the briars, the more pungent the smell became.

In a small clearing I saw her, gasping in the tall grass: a red wolf with a sucking gunshot wound on the right side of her ribcage. Her tongue lolled as she panted, eyeing me in agony and terror. The buzzards flocked closer. I had not heard any gunfire, so she must have traveled there from quite some distance away, that gaping hole burning in her side, oozing blood into the weeds.

"I'm sorry, girl," I said, crouching down to her level. "You are not supposed to be here any longer. Not for a century or more." She panted and panted as the buzzards advanced. Nearby, I saw a tight stand of Siberian larch. *I believe we are here.*

And indeed we were.

Emily had undersold how burned out and desiccated the house was on the outside. It appeared as though the brambles and briars would overtake it within the decade. Walking the perimeter, I noticed that a basement window had been recently replaced with fresh safety glass. The calking was still smooth all around it. I kicked at the window with the heel of my left boot several times, and managed to start a small crack in the thick, barely translucent glass. I kicked it a few more times, and the fissure grew wider. *Maybe that'll give someone a fighting chance someday,* I thought. *Who knows?*

I headed on inside.

The interior was nice enough, I guess. Quaint, but drab. "Hello?" I shouted, but heard nothing in return. I saw a pair of green sandals by the door. I also could not help but notice scratches and gouges in the frame around the door, and bloodstains on the hardwood floor below it. "Anybody home?" I asked, a bit louder this time. Still no response. Cautiously, I laid my bags in the foyer.

From there, I entered what I took to be the parlor, then walked down a short hallway to the living room. Lying on her back across one of two couches was a girl, sixteen tops, holding a small, round mirror above her face. She was dressed exactly as Emily had been when I first met her. Exactly, but for the color of her plastic ankle bracelet. The girl breathed heavily and rapidly, reminding me instantly of the dying wolf I had seen outside. I wondered if she was having an anxiety attack.

I cleared my throat, and she shot up quickly with a tiny squeal. She dropped the mirror to the floor and brushed her long, curly red hair away from her face.

She sat cross-legged, panting, looking furtively about. There was no one else around, as far as I could tell.

"Hi there," I said. "How are you?" Pause. "May I sit?"

She nodded, indicating space on the couch. I sat. The walls of the room contained no art, only framed mirrors. It was drafty, damp, and there was no fire in the fireplace. I doubt that there had been one in quite a while.

"Is it like this always?"

She nodded.

"Figured." I indicated another doorway to the left. "That's the kitchen?" I asked. She nodded again. She nodded a lot. There was another door leading off the living room. It was shut tight. Beside it, a key dangled from a hook on the wall.

"This is pretty much what I anticipated," I said. "Although, I must say, I did not expect you."

"I didn't expect *you*," she replied.

"Apologies," I said. "I didn't mean to interrupt." She shrugged. "This isn't bad. I mean, to be honest, it is really not that bad at all. I certainly expected a bit worse."

"Worse?"

"Like, more ghoulish or some shit. But that's all right. I can always spice it up a bit once the drafting starts. Really make it pop in revision. You know?"

"Um... no."

"Lay on the drama. Give the people what they want. Blood and screwing, that's what they want." She nodded. "I am not just here for the facts; I'm here for the truth. Okay?"

"Okay," she replied.

"I will tell you the truth, little bean. If I'm the one bleeding words onto the page, it's *my* story. My words, my lens. *That* is the truth." She nodded again.

We sat in silence for a bit. I heard neither creak nor peep from the rest of the house.

"So..." I asked finally. "What brought you here?"

"What brought YOU here?"

"I'm writing a book."

"That's not important."

"I'm getting paid to write a book."

"Fuck you!" For no evident reason, she leaned in and tried to kiss me. I respectfully declined. She backed away, looking shocked. "You think I'm ugly!"

"I absolutely do not."

Outside grew ever darker. A storm began to brew, and the windows rattled from the wind.

"Emily kisses me," the girl said, pouting.

"I'm sure she does." Pause. "Where is Emily now?"

"Where is Emily now… In our bedroom."

"Upstairs?"

"Upstairs."

"And why aren't you there?"

"She wanted to be with herself." Pause. "And I'm not Emily." Pause. "Yet."

I did not realize at first, but at this point she was looking right over my shoulder, sour-faced and annoyed. She shouted past me, "No one is impressed, you boring thing!"

I turned around and was startled to see a faceless figure in the doorway, half obscured by shadow. The figure's head was covered in what I could best describe as a tattered, old wedding veil. I could not see through it at all, and wondered how she could possibly see out. She bobbed her head from side to side like blind musicians do.

"The fuck is that?!" I shouted.

"Ignore her," the girl said. "She just wants attention."

I stood up and faced the figure, retrieving my small notebook and pen from my jacket pocket. I tried speaking to the shrouded woman, but she just bobbed her head in silence. Then she vanished into the darkness of the hall. The girl cackled at me.

"I told you to ignore her!" she said, falling into a fit of giggles. I plopped back down on the couch.

What am I doing here… seriously… what am I doing in this place…

"Who is this, baby?" a woman's voice asked from behind me. "A new friend?"

I turned my head again to see another woman standing in the doorway. Mid-thirties for sure, smartly dressed, pristine manicure and pedicure, tasteful gold jewelry, flawless make-up. Her dark hair lay in a perfect, straight, shoulder-length bob, her make-up flawless as if she had just come fresh from the salon. Her demeanor was confident, bordering on macho. She was flushed and slightly out of breath, sizing me up before taking a seat on the couch next to the girl.

"A new friend," the girl confirmed, beaming at the sight of her, cuddling close and resting her head on the woman's shoulder.

"Hello, new friend."

I was not prepared.

"Hello, Ms. Conlin."

"So formal," she replied.

"It's... good to see you, Emily."

"Have we met?"

"You could say."

Emily's face darkened, but then she smiled.

"How wonderful. Do you have news for me?"

"That's not why I am here," I replied. "I just needed a broader perspective." I held up my notebook and pen.

"Ah. Well, be careful. It can be treacherous. And we want you to write nice things about us."

"Impartial field research," I said. "That is the only reason I'm here."

"Fair enough. I just hope you don't get cold feet, new friend. You do strike me as the curious type."

The shrouded woman entered from the kitchen, awkwardly carrying a tray of biscuits and cups. I had not noticed it before, but her left hand was bloodied and bandaged into a ball. I stood to help, but Emily waved her hand for me to sit down. The shrouded woman set the tray on the other couch, then went back into the kitchen. The girl giggled and Emily shushed her with a devious grin.

A moment later, the woman returned, struggling to carry the small but heavy coffee table from the parlor. I stood to take the table from her. I set the coffee table on the floor between the couches, and the shrouded woman placed the tray clumsily upon it, the cups and saucers rattling. She picked the small mirror off the floor and placed it on the coffee table as well.

From the kitchen came another lady, late-sixties/early seventies, carrying a carafe of tea. She smiled at me, polite but strained, and set the carafe next to the biscuits and cups. Also on the tea tray were two serrated knives.

"Good afternoon, young man," the lady said, taking a seat next to the shrouded woman on the other couch. "I thought I heard someone on the porch earlier."

"You would tell me to leave immediately," I said, "but I wouldn't have come if that sort of advice mattered to me."

The older lady smiled and nodded.

"Of course," she said. "Of course."

"What happened to her hand?" I asked, indicating the shrouded woman. The shrouded woman covered her bandaged hand with her sleeve.

"It doesn't matter anymore," the other lady replied.

"Doesn't matter anymore," the girl agreed.

"Can't you show her some sympathy?" I asked.

All three of them chuckled at me. "That is enough for you, boring thing," Emily said to the shrouded woman. *Guess that answers that question.*

"Why don't you go rest a bit, darling," said the older lady to the shrouded woman, patting her gently on the arm. The shrouded woman stood and shuffled away.

The older lady smiled pleasantly at me but did not speak, the sole of her left shoe tapping softly on the hardwood floor. Emily and the girl cuddled and kissed, whispering and giggling to one another, unbothered by my presence on the other end of the couch. Emily wrapped the wool scarf loosely about the girl's neck.

I poured tea from the carafe into the four ceramic cups, which steamed and bubbled. Just then, I noticed two large, dark stains on the hardwood floor in front of the fireplace.

"Looks like something bad went down here," I said.

"I am quite sure it was nothing to write about," said Emily.

"Mistakes can happen," the older lady said, looking briefly over toward Emily. "It can't be helped."

I considered writing "mistakes can happen" in my notebook, but figured I would remember it.

"What do you know about this place?" Emily asked me.

I picked up a serrated knife from the tray, cut the biscuit in half and took a bite, skipping the marmalade. "I don't know much," I admitted. "Not nearly enough." I picked up a cup of tea. The girl sat up and did as well.

"Careful, it's hot," Emily said. She was right.

I indicated the closed door. "I am curious about the cellar."

"There is a fruit cellar," the older lady said. "Fresh pickings. Quite delicious."

"How about the cold storage in back?"

"There's nothing for you there," Emily said.

"What about for you?"

"I don't go there. The smell does not suit me."

"Are there others about?" I asked. "I might like to meet them."

"They are...here and there," Emily said.

"The Dog is in the cellar," the girl said. "You should *definitely avoid him.*"

Suddenly, we heard music playing from down the hall—Billie Holiday singing "Comes Love." The sound of wingtips tapping along the wood floors grew closer and closer. A voice sang along:

"Don't try hiding, cuz there isn't any use / You start sliding when your heart turns on the juice..."

"He loves this song," the older lady said.

"He does," said the girl, nodding.

"Comes a headache you can lose it in a day / comes a toothache, see your dentist right away / Comes love, nothing

can be doooone…"

A man sauntered in, swigging from a bottle of *Chateau le Thys*. Lean, muscular build, thick black hair just starting to gray at the temples, well-dressed but disheveled, in a black suit with a white pressed shirt unbuttoned to the chest.

"Well, hello there," he said when he saw me.

"Hello," I replied.

He plopped down on the sofa next to the older lady.

"You're new," he said to me.

"So far."

"Dibs!" he shouted, throwing up his hand.

"Show some manners," Emily said pointedly.

The man rolled his eyes and took another belt of wine. "Psh. You used to be fun, Emily."

"No, I did not."

I blew on my tea and took a sip. It was sweetened with what tasted like raw sugar, balanced with lemon. There was also a sharply bitter undertone to the flavor that struck me as very familiar, but I just could not quite place what it was. I took another sip. Vague recognition.

"He is writing a book about us," the girl said.

"Oh, how exciting," the man said. "Tell him about the day we met, Emily. And how you were such a delicate little—"

"Manners!"

"MANNERS!" the girl echoed.

"—*individual* person," the man said with a smirk. "Or you could write about how The Dog plunged that little girl's honey pot 'til she fell unconscious."

Emily, the man, and the older lady all laughed heartily. The girl pouted. *Hilarious.*

"It doesn't matter," the girl said, irritated, her arms crossed. "The Dog bores me now."

"And yet, you keep going down there to give him treats."

The girl leapt up and screamed, "I will fucking KILL YOU!!!"

She grabbed a knife from the table and pointed it at him. The man guffawed and slapped his knee. He took another gulp of wine and offered it to her. She drank, still frowning, and handed the bottle back to him.

"Sit, please, sweet angel," Emily said. The girl sat back down, returning the knife to its tray. I wrote all this down.

"The Dog is your other, I take it?"

"Or I'm his," the man replied with a shrug. "Whatever. It's all the same."

"Do you have news for us?" the older lady asked me. "How is Kurtis?"

"He blew his head off with a shotgun," I replied. The man and the older lady both howled with laughter. Emily looked upset, even though I had assumed that she already knew.

"Okay," the man said, still laughing. He looked over at Emily with a Cheshire grin, "So then... how is—"

"Stop now," Emily said. "I don't want to hear this."

"Come on, Em, you have always been a curious girl."

"STOP. NOW."

"Enough!" said the red-haired girl.

"Be honest," the man said, clearly enjoying getting under Emily's skin. "Is she like Kurtis now?"

"Stop it!"

"STOP IT!" the girl shouted.

"Is she dead?" he asked me.

"If she's dead, I do not want to know!" Emily screamed.

The girl flapped her hands nervously, launching daggers at the man with her eyes. He smiled in reply. I really liked his smile, shit-eating though it was.

"She is not dead," I said.

"Ah," the man said, lifting his bottle in salute. "Well, good for her."

Emily poured the young girl another cup of tea, which she drank quickly. I finished mine, and it was then that I noticed that only the girl and I were drinking tea. In fact, the older lady lifted the top of the carafe and poured the two undrunk cups back into it. I put my empty cup down. The aftertaste lingered, bitter and familiar.

"How many others are here?" I asked.

"Many and few," the older lady said.

"We could introduce you," the man said to me. "There is always time."

"Time enough," Emily agreed.

"Time enough…" the girl yawned. She set her cup down.

"Oh my, it is so late!" Emily said.

"Soooo late…" the girl slurred. She was fading fast. And suddenly.

Though I could not imagine that it was really all that late, it was completely dark outside. The wind rattled the windows, and rain began to fall at last. The girl leaned into Emily's arms and fell asleep, her head resting on Emily's shoulder. Emily wrapped her arms around her, stroking her fire-red curls. She cuddled the sleeping girl for a minute or two. Then she looked over to the man.

"Would you be the bestest buddy pal in the whole wide world and please carry my sweet angel upstairs?"

"With pleasure," he sighed. "Of course."

He stood up, polished off his wine, set the empty bottle on the coffee table, then scooped the girl into his arms. The white wool scarf fell from her neck to the floor. Emily picked it up and draped it across the armrest of her side of the couch.

"To MY room," Emily said. "No others."

"I could take her downstairs," he said. "She likes it down there."

"Upstairs. To my room."

"You used to be fun, Emily."

"That is not true and you know it."

The man bowed his head in my direction. "Good night, hand-some."

Now that's funny.

As he walked past me, carrying the girl limp in his arms, I

said, "Billie sends her regards." He stopped cold. After a moment's pause, he exited to the hallway, not quite as jauntily as when he had entered.

Without a word, the older lady gathered the uneaten biscuits and marmalade, the mirror, the bottle, and all but my teacup onto the tray. She also left the carafe and both serrated knives. She smiled and nodded to Emily and me, her snow-white hair bobbing lightly in her face. Then she exited into the kitchen.

We were alone, but we did not speak. We listened to the rain instead. I set my spiral notebook down on the table and put my pen in my jacket pocket.

"It is odd," she said finally. "You feel you have spent time with me before. But I have never met you until now."

"How are you getting on? Any regrets?"

"There was never any doubt in my mind I would come in some day."

"*'C'mon, Em, quit yer foolin' around,*" I said, doing my best Seth impersonation. It was not very good.

"I miss him," she said. "I miss a lot of things. I miss the touch of wind and the morning dew. I miss the swimming hole in summer, even though I can't swim. I miss the first snow of winter, and the feel of grass under my feet in spring." She glided her bare soles softly across the hardwood floor. "I miss a lot."

"Do you want me to tell you about her?" I asked. "I will if you want me to, but it's up to you."

"I don't know," she said. "I don't know which one I was. I don't know which one I am." Pause. "She's... pretty?"

"Yep."

"But not as pretty as I wish she was."

"If you say so."

Emily poured me another cup of tea. I could still taste the lingering bitterness of the last cup, but I took a sip.

"So... whose story is this?" she asked. "Emily's? Mine? Yours?"

"It is a story about a cage, and the people who love it."

"But isn't that every story?"

"It sure is."

We paused, listening to the rain again.

Finally, I said, "You need to let her go, Emily."

"What?! She left ME!"

"No, I mean the little girl upstairs. Let her go before—"

"You can't take her from me."

"I am just writing a book, Emily."

"Then write your stupid book," she spat. "It's not like I'LL ever get a chance to read it. But don't forget your role in all this, new friend. You are just a writer. Just a hack writer. A ghost. A phantom. Don't fancy yourself a liberator."

"'*All artists*,'" I said, quoting Edwidge Danticat, "'*writers among them, have stories that haunt and obsess them.*'"

"Is that what this is for you?" she asked. "A story that haunts and obsesses you?"

"We shall see," I replied. "It's early yet."

"It's later than you think it is," she said.

"You may be right."

I lifted the cup to my lips for another sip of tea, but my face began to feel hot and prickly. My stomach churned. I felt dizzy and nauseated. Double vision.

"I...I..."

I looked at my left hand shaking. The cup fell to the table. It spilled but did not break. She lifted my teacup to her face to inspect it, and in that moment, I realized what that bitter flavor was.

"You'll pay..." I slurred, angry at her, but more at myself for being so careless, and for not immediately recognizing *the taste of fucking Phenobarbital.*

"That took longer than it should have," she said, setting the cup down. "But you are bigger than she is."

"You'll suffer..." I growled, black balloons exploding in my eyes as I struggled to maintain. "I will... make you... suffer..."

"All in good time."

I leaned back on the couch, struggling to breathe, still conscious, but feeling like a wet sack of gravel. Through the slits of my eyelids, I saw her saunter over to the door to the cellar, unlock the door, and hang the key back on its hook. She opened the door wide and said, "It's a treat, boy! Come get the treat!" I might have been able to move if I really tried, but it just didn't seem worth the effort. She bent down and kissed me on the lips. "Goodnight, Mr. Writer. Dream good things about us." She shut my eyes with her fingers, and all was dark.

All Was Dark

"Hold the moon, my dear
  Steal it clearly feeling healed
  Leering through the clearing field
  Nearly keeping sealed in fear"
Eyes closed, halfway between awake and asleep. I hear a
voice singing softly to me. Fingertips caress my hair.
  "Old, the morning dear
  Fear it, keep it sealed in steel
  Praise it happening as often
  Scream and scrape the lid of my coffin"
Warmth. Scent of an aged cedar chest. Someone has covered
me in a quilt. Soft fingers against my cheek. Singing…
  "Leering through the clearing field
  Nearly keeping sealed in fear
  Old, the morning dear
  Fear it, keep it sealed in steel"
Recognize the voice. It is the voice of the older lady, soft and
warm. Life is a queer nightmare.
  "Hold the moon my dear
  Steal it clearly feeling healed
  Praise it happening as often
  Scream and scrape the lid of my coffin"
Thought I had written this song. D# to G#, E with an A
sympathetic drone. A lullaby of death. Melodies float in space
to be captured like fireflies…
  "Hold the moon my dear…

Hold the moon my dear...
Hold the moon my dear...
Hold the moon my dear..."

Open my eyes to see tattered, opaque shroud and a bandaged, bloody hand. Other hand, soft and old, caresses my cheek one last time.

"Sleep..." the figure whispers, and fades into shadow. Darkness again.

Consciousness continued to ebb and flow, but I did not open my eyes.

At some point, I felt the pressure of body weight on my legs. I felt my belt unbuckling and the top button of my jeans becoming unfastened. I opened my eyes to see the red-haired girl straddling me, staring down, attempting to mimic the look on my heretofore sleeping face. Seeing my eyes open, she refastened my pants, rebuckled my belt, and crawled back from me, sitting cross-legged on the other side of the couch. She wore an off-white mulberry silk slip, her wild, dark ginger hair even more tussled than before, face flushed, jade irises flickering in the light of kerosene lamps on the mantle above the cold, stone hearth. I felt woozy and less than oriented, my head not quite stable in its position on my neck. I had to figure that she felt the same.

I sat up, my left shoulder throbbing. I patted myself down for my spiral notebook. My jacket pocket was empty of both notebook and pen.

When did I put my jacket back on?

"Shit," I said. "She took it, didn't she."

"She took it," the girl replied, fiddling with her plastic, pine-green anklet. Pause. "Do you want to hear a story?"

"Yes."

"Once upon a time," she said, "there was a musician. And he was married to a beautiful lady. One day, the musician and his beautiful wife were picnicking in a beautiful glen, and he played a beautiful song. As he played, she danced in the tall grass, beautifully. Suddenly, a venomous viper sprang up from the tall grass and bit her toes! She screamed in agony as the venom coursed through her veins. Then she died, and was dragged straight down to Hell. The end."

"I love that story."

"Of course you do. Everyone does."

"There is a lot of truth there."

"Everyone loves the truth."

"You should go. You don't need to stay here."

"Stay here," she said, looking around on the floor in front and behind the couch. The quilt lay on the floor. Nothing on the coffee table save the carafe, my chipped teacup, and two serrated knives. The door to the cellar was closed and locked again.

"I am. I'm going to. I have work to do."

"Work to do. Where has my scarf gone to?"

"But you can run."

"I can't."

"Run back home. Get out there."

"They were cruel to me out there."

"They are cruel to you in here."

"Not like out there. Emily loves me."

"Emily only loves Emily."

"I'm working on that."

"You're foolish, little bean."

"She cares for me."

"Do you know where Down Pattersons is? Near Burlington?"

"I don't even know *what* that is."

"It's nearby. You probably passed through it to get here."

"I jumped from a moving car."

"Someone will help you there."

"No one will help me. No one will ever help me."

"I know Emily out there," I said. "I *know* her. Perhaps she would care for you."

She stared at me; mouth slightly agape.

"Do… do you think?"

"Occasionally."

"They were so vicious to me out there."

"Were they now?"

"They did horrible, vicious, cruel things to me."

"Fantastic!" From nervous habit, I patted myself down again for the notebook. *It's not there, dumbass.* "I need paper." My head was filled with poison clouds. It began to throb, particularly the left side. My left nostril clogged with dried blood.

"Fantastic."

"And a pen." I could hear my heartbeat growing louder in my ears. *Thump… thump… thump…* "Can you tell me what they did to you? Everything? In specific, excruciating detail?"

Thump… thump… thump…

"Spare no drop of blood?"

Like a skull against wooden stairs…

"Not a drop."

Thump… thump… thump…

"The dark things deep down?"

"That is all I care about," I said, clutching my forehead. "That's all I have *ever* cared about."

"If I tell you all the specific details of the cruel things they did to me," she said, "exactly, explicitly, excruciatingly, will you masturbate?"

Thump… thump… thump…

"I'll write a book."

Thump…

"You echo me."

Thump…

My eyes adjusted to the dim light, and I saw that my book bag and duffle were by the fireplace under a spattering of blood on the wall, still fresh enough to glisten. I wondered how they got there. *At least I have notebooks now.*

"What is your name, little girl?" *Thump.* "You can tell me the truth."

On the stone hearth of the cold fireplace lay the smashed remnants of my black ink pen. *Oh right. That is where it fell.*

"The truth."

"What's your name? And don't tell me that it doesn't matter anymore."

"It doesn't matter anymore."

"Don't tell me that. What is your name?"

"It doesn't matter."

"What name did they give you out there?"

"They were cruel to me out there."

"What cruel name did they give you out there, little girl?"

"It doesn't matter anymore."

"What's your goddamn name?"

"Whatever *she* wants to call me."

"What name did the cruel people give you?"

"Make you come, make you cry, make you die," she whimpered, yanking at her hair with both fists. "I have talents."

"Tell me your name!"

"I am a sweet, sweet angel."

"What's your real name?"

"Who's to say that it's even my real name?"

"Your outside name."

"I don't go outside anymore."

"What was the name?"

"Gone for good."

"Tell me!"

"ELIZA!"

Pause.

What the fuck...

"That's ridiculous."

"Yes."

Oh HELL no...

"That can't possibly be true."

"It's what they called me."

"Stop lying."

"I'm truthful."

The clouds in my head swirled and got darker...

"I can't accept that!"

My heart thumped louder...

"That's what it was!"

...the angrier I became.

"You're wrong!"

"Wrong about my name?!"

"Wrong!"

"It was Eliza!"

Too on-the-nose!

"That is... bad writing! Pick something better!"

The shrouded woman shuffled in from the hallway. Both of her hands were now bandaged and bloody.

"Oh, look!" the girl exclaimed, throwing up her arms in a grand display. "Just on cue. It was the boring thing's cue to enter, so she entered."

"You," I shouted at the shrouded woman. "Tell me her name." Silence. "Tell me her REAL name!" Silence. "Tell me YOUR name!"

"Don't yell at her!" the girl said. "She doesn't remember!"

"Come here!"

The shrouded woman shuffled over to me. I sat her down on the couch and knelt on the floor in front of her. The girl panicked and began fanning her face with both hands.

"Oh no, no no no no no no no," the girl said, her voice cracking. "You can't do that to her!" I lifted the shroud from the woman's face. "Nooooo," the girl cried, "please...please don't do that!" She rocked back and forth, hitting herself on the head and pulling at her hair.

I will be damned...

The woman looked exactly like the older lady, the lady in the white blouse with sensible shoes. Exactly. Only *harmed*. Damaged. Her face was wrapped in blood-soaked rags, as if she had been repeatedly stabbed in the face—bloody circles on dirty bandages green with infection, where eyes should have been. Eliza shrieked pitifully and buried her face in the couch cushion.

All I could think to say to the woman was, "Why?"

"She..." the woman droned in monotone. "She didn't want me... she didn't want me looking... She didn't want me looking at her... She didn't want me looking like her... anymore..."

Vomit rose from my stomach as my anger swelled. I swallowed them both back and stood.

"Get up."

"Please, no!" Eliza cried, standing up as well, her hands folded in front of her.

"GET. UP."

The woman did not respond. I lifted her to a standing position.

"Don't make her!"

"Run now."

"You can't make her!"

"Go on," I said to the woman. "Leave!"

"Please don't do this!" Eliza screamed.

I picked up one of the knives from the coffee table and held the flat metal blade against the woman's cheek. No response.

"Go, or I will carve the rest of it off."

The woman did not move. She just stood there, her head bobbing back and forth. I grabbed her by the collar of her tattered blouse and dragged her down the hall.

"Stop!!! Please!!!" Eliza cried, chasing after.

Passing through the parlor, I bumped into the Gramophone by accident. The needle scraped across *Body and Soul*. The woman neither cooperated nor resisted as I dragged her into the foyer and threw open the door. She merely acquiesced.

"Go now," I said to the woman. "Run. Scream for help. Someone from Down Pattersons will come for you. NOW!"

I pushed the woman out the front door and shut it behind her.

"How could you?!" Eliza shrieked. "YOU'VE KILLED HER!"

"I set her free."

"THERE IS NO DIFFERENCE!!!"

I pointed at the green sandals by the wall with my knife.

"Put your shoes on," I said. "We're leaving too."

"NO!" she cried.

"Goddamn it! I need my fucking bags!"

Stomping back down the hall toward the living room I could hear pounding, rattling, and the screams of multiple voices from upstairs. *Fighting... torture... fucking... murder... it's all the same to the clam...*

Storming into the living room I found Emily standing between me and my bags. Like the girl, she wore an off-white mulberry silk slip, but with a matching short silk night robe as well. Her face was severe, and fearful. She eyed the knife in my hand.

"Move, Emily."

"What's going on?"

"He killed her!" Eliza sobbed, trailing behind me.

"Fine!" Emily said with an exaggerated shrug. "Who cares!"

"He pushed her out the door!" the girl cried. Emily's face blanched.

"Oh my GOD!"

My skull was a throbbing, echoing chamber of cacophony and inchoate rage. I wanted to smash Emily's face against the stone hearth of the cold, dead fireplace. Instead, I grabbed the red-haired girl around the shoulders with my right arm and held the serrated blade of the knife under her chin.

"I'm taking her too."

"You can't have her!!!"

"Can't have her!" the girl wailed.

"What's her name, Emily?"

"What?!"

I began inching backward toward the doorway to the hall, holding the trembling girl to my chest.

"What is her name?"

"Why are you doing this to me?!?!" Emily shouted, her voice cracking.

"NAME!"

"Her name is...is...sweetest baby!"

"Goodbye, Emily."

"EMILY!" Eliza cried, reaching out for her.

"I'll take you to Emily," I said.

"NO!" Emily screamed. "You can't! She's selfish! I'm kind!"

From the hallway ran the older lady in a fluffy, pink house-coat with matching slippers, and the man, shirtless and sweaty in black dress slacks and gold-tipped socks.

"What in Hell?!" the man shouted.

"Not just yet," I growled through my teeth, breathing heavily. I could not fully process what I was doing, or why. "All in good time."

"Where is she?!" the older lady screamed.

"Say goodbye."

"WHERE IS SHE?!?!?!"

"She's gone," I spat. "You're alone. Make your peace with that."

"He threw her out the door!" Eliza blubbered.

The woman's face contorted in abject rage and despair. She grabbed the sides of her head and screamed—

"KIIIIIIIIIIIIIIIIILLLLLLLLLLLLL HIIIIIIIIIIIIIIIMMMMMMMMM!!!!!"

The man lunged toward the coffee table and grabbed the other knife. I threw Eliza to the floor. The man charged at me, swinging his knife overhead like an idiot who should have known better. I buried mine deep in his exposed stomach.

He groaned in shock and agony, crumpling to the floor, bringing me down to the floor with him. His knife clattered across the hardwood. The older lady collapsed to the floor as well, sobbing and wailing. I could feel the man's hot blood spurting up my forearm. He gurgled and moaned as quarts hemorrhaged from his mouth. I retched sugar lemon tea and

Phenobarbital from mine.

"I'm sorry," I whispered, my throat knotted, tears burning in my eyes. "I'm so sorry." He only gurgled in reply.

Panicking, I tried to dislodge the serrated knife from him, but it was caught on something visceral. The more I pulled the more it snagged, sawing into him, up, then side to side. *Sign of the Cross. Father, son, etc.* More blood spurted from his mouth and his guts.

He gripped my right shoulder, his eyes deep crimson with burst vessels, his blanched face awash in sweat, tears, and blood.

"*Ah wun mah mommuh...*" he whined, pleading. "*Uh wunn muh mahmmuh...*"

The pool of blood around us grew wider in every direction. I thought about lifting him and carrying him outside. Scream for help, hope someone can come in time to save him.

That is not the deal, I thought. *That would be a double-cross.*

That brief flight of fancy was for naught anyway, as he puked out a gallon of blood down the front of me, gasped, and then collapsed into my shoulder, still gushing. Lights out. He was dead.

Numb.

I was so numb I could just faintly hear the shrieking all around me. I was so numb I could barely feel the blade of the other serrated knife pressing against my neck.

"This ends now," Emily hissed. I could have probably grabbed her wrist and snatched it from her, but with my dominant hand stuck, she had the advantage. It hardly seemed worth the effort anyway.

The older lady sobbed in anguish, writhing on the floor.

"*Kill him...kill him...*"

"Just step away," I said to Emily.

"I can't," she replied. "I never will."

Eliza sobbed as well, doubled over on her knees.

"Come with me," I said, extending my one free hand toward the girl. "We can make it."

She reached meekly toward my hand, and Emily slashed at her with the knife. Eliza recoiled in terror and shame.

"No one else is going through that door," Emily said, panting.

"Never?" Eliza whimpered.

"Not ever," Emily seethed.

I finally managed to wriggle the knife free from the dead man's guts. Spurt and spillage. Emily pressed the serrated blade harder into my flesh and I tossed the knife onto the left-side couch. It spattered the cushions with blood and black bile.

Emily pointed her knife toward Eliza.

"Crawl, baby," Emily said. "Crawl to me like you do." Like a weeping alligator, Eliza crawled across the hardwood floor through the ever-widening pool of blood, her dark ginger curls obscuring her blotchy, tear-drenched face.

"Please, Emily..." Eliza cried, crawling toward her, the hem of her mulberry silk slip soaked in blood, her right knee raw and tender. "Please... *I love you.*"

"Sit up," Emily said. Eliza sat up on her knees. "Open your mouth. Wide." She did. Emily grabbed the carafe from the coffee table and poured cold, laced tea down the sobbing girl's throat. Eliza sputtered and coughed.

Emily thrust the carafe toward me. "Finish it." From the weight I guessed it was still nearly a quarter full.

"Probably enough to kill me here," I said.

"We will see about that."

I proceeded to gulp down the cold, bitter brew, gagging and choking once or twice. *Well, I won't be having any seizures at least.*

"Now," Emily announced, "we are all going down to the cellar."

"YEEESSS!" the older lady hollered, still lying on the floor. "Feed him to the fucking DOG!!!"

"I don't mind dogs," I said.

"DIE!!!" she screeched at me.

"We're acquainted."

Well acquainted.

"You're a LIAR! That is all that you are!"

In truth, I cannot dispute that.

Eliza and the older lady got up from the floor, both still crying. Emily kicked the quilt at me. I caught it. She pointed at the dead man on the floor with her knife.

"This is your mess, you stupid fucking twat," Emily said to me. "You clean it up. Wrap him and carry him down. Now."

"Kill him for this..." the older lady blubbered. "Kill him..."

"All in good time," Emily said. She picked up the other knife from the couch and walked to the cellar door.

"Drag him t-to the fucking cellar," the lady groaned. "Feed him to the f-fucking Dog..."

"We are all going down," Emily said, unlocking the door and dropping the key into the pocket of her silk nightrobe. "All the way down."

Down and Down and Down and Down and Down

Weight of the dead man on my left shoulder, blood-drenched quilt leaking down my back. Emily locks cellar door behind me. "Move" she says, knife blade in my right shoulder. Head swimming in gray haze as I navigate narrow cellar stairway. Dark dirigibles exploding in my eyes. Thick boots on wooden steps *thump... thump... thump*. Bottom of stairs, unseen, old lady wails and moans, girl sniffles and sobs. *'And I, who had my head with horror bound, said "Master, what is this which now I hear?"'* On an ancient, wind-up Gramophone warped vinyl *Body and Soul* warbles at half-speed. Old lady groans along in time.

"*Myyyyyy daaaaaayssss haaaaaaave grooooooown sooooo lonelyyyyyyyy...*"

Cold chill hangs, vague stench of death wafts from deep in back. Stomach churns. Bottom of stairs now seen, growing gray light of kerosene lamps. Slow, warbling voices—

"*Fooooor youuuuuu I cryyyyyyyy...*"

Drop the dead man to cold cement floor with a wet *thump. Thump.*

"*Fooooor youuuuuu dearrrrr oooonlyyyyyyyy...*"

"Dog looks exactly like him," Emily says. No Dog in sight. Shape moves in periphery. Growling and blood gurgling, just out of sight. "He's all yours!" Emily shouts to the shadows. "Use once and destroy." About the room ugly electric lamp lights balance awkwardly on twisted, bendable stems. Wood and steel workbenches. *'But, I say, where are the instruments of torture?'* I think, because Jean-Paul thought. *'The racks and red-hot pincers and all the other paraphernalia?'* Instead, bowls of dark berries, all fresh pickings, and uncorked bottles, half-drunk and half-full. Piles of powders and pills, green gel caps and razor blades. *I could live here. I could live here a while.* Shape moves about the space, knocks into lights, casting grim shadows across desiccated stone walls rotting like septic flesh. Drugs in my system make rotting walls pulsate and ooze. Bowls of fresh fruit entice my twisting stomach. *Walked entire perimeter of this house before entering. Not a garden to be seen among the brambles and briars. Whither comes the fruit?* Menacing flash of silver screwdriver shines in lamplight. "Use once and destroy." On the floor, on knees and doubled over, singing and moaning old lady. Pink house coat and matching slippers. Serrated knife driven deep into her soft belly. Ever-widening pool of blood surrounds her. Hot blood steams and hisses on cold cement floor.

"Lot of blood," Emily says. "Lot of blood and screwing. Just an observation."

I black out.

Come to against stone wall, wrists bent inward under chin, shivering from cold and blood-pressure drop. Dominant hand stained red. Warped vinyl warbles half-speed. Man wrapped in quilt bled out dead. Old woman bleeding, still bleeding, still bleeding. Faintly singing. Singing and bleeding. Knocked lights, casting shadows. Growling closer. Growing closer. "Use once and destroy." Hard heel boots clack against cement. Emily guzzles wine with one hand, other hand jerks under Eliza's blood-drenched silk slip. Girl pants, gasps, and squeals.

"Say you're my girl," Emily purrs, licking girl's cheek, biting her neck. "Say it, I'll let you come."

"I'm your girl!" Eliza whimpers, trembling. "I'm your baby angel girl! Make me come, Mommy, pleeeeeeease!!!"

Push myself upright. Toward me he lurches from shadows like a lesser god, The Dog, like the man I killed, lean and taut.

A faltering limp to his strut. Muscles pulse and throb. Dark, stained jeans and silver-tipped cowboy boots. Thick black hair mussed and wild, graying at temples red and stiff with dried blood. Eyelids purple and bruised, smeared and running with black mascara. Nose smashed, pouring blood down his face and torso, *CRAWL* carved into bare chest black and infected.

"You want it," he hisses at me.

"All in good time."

"You wanna fuck... Your body is currency..."

Scoop pulped fruit and goo of green gel caps into my dominant hand. He feeds, grinning crimson, chipped teeth stained with blood, berries, and dark red wine. He kisses me wet and hard, copper and sweet. He bites me. I bite him back.

"Useful for our purposes," he growls, grinning, grabbing me down below. My arsenal. Useful. Not an exorcism. Like draining a septic wound. I grab his wrist and smile.

"All in good time."

Eliza screams in ecstasy, grinding against Emily's fingers within her slip, convulsing in climax. Emily lifts girl's trembling young body onto wood work table like a sacrifice. Rolls onto her back cooing and writhing.

"I love you..." girl shudders. "I love you..."

Dog advances. I advance. Cut fat rails of powder and crushed pills. Slit gel caps down the middle. Grab wine bottles red and white and blush. We all snort. We all lick. We all gulp.

"People say the house should be bulldozed," Emily says licking wet fingers. "Then they vanish. Screaming and jabbering. Nearly mute. Drenched in blood."

"Drenched in blood."

"Stay away from that house..."

Scooping berries, all fresh pickings, squished and quite delicious. *Whither comes the fruit?* She feeds her and she feeds me and she feeds him and he feeds her and I feed them. Filthy fingers licked clean.

"Always been a curious girl. The house is haunted by me."

"Porch floorboards creaked under my feet," Eliza says, still on her back. Emily scoops berries and powders and feeds her. Dark red stains on flushed cheeks and mulberry silk.

"You are a curious girl."

"Always have been."

"Hello there, young lady," Emily says and kisses her. Old lady on the floor tries to pull the knife from her stomach. Nauseating groan. Knife snagged and caught in viscera. Sawing. *Father, son, etc.* Pink housecoat soaked red. Knife comes free with a rip, spurt and spill. Dog picks it up. Now has a knife and a screwdriver. Hands occupied. I scoop berries and pills and feed him. He licks my hand. Bites the hand that feeds.

"What is your name?" Eliza asks. Sits up, still quivering from cold chill and orgasm. Gulps white wine.

"Doesn't matter anymore," Emily says.

"My name is Emily Conlin," Eliza says.

"It doesn't matter anymore."

"It matters to me."

"Do you know yourself then?"

"I should hope so."

"I wish nothing but the best for your sweet girl," The Dog snarls.

"My sweet girl?"

"For you. Sweet girl," Emily says, kisses Eliza again. "Should we leave the boys be, baby? Let The Dog feast on flesh? Should we go upstairs? Now? You and me? To the circle room?" Eliza whimpers and looks at me. Jade irises surrounding dilated pupils.

"I'm just curious," she whispers.

"Of course you are!" The Dog yells.

"Curiosity is not a crime," I say. "*I will take you*" I mouth in silence.

"GUILTY, you wretch!" hollers The Dog.

Loud banging from inside cold storage. Muffled screams.

"Sour meat my dear."

"It doesn't matter anymore."

Emily hands The Dog her knife. Two knives and a screwdriver. Only odd numbers. Rather cruel.

Old lady gasps one last time. Bleed out. Bled out. Blood out. Dead.

Pounding from cold storage door again. Muffled shouting. Emily collapses at the waist and screams. Wrenching, piercing.

"AAAAAAAAAAAAAAAAAAAAAAAAAAAAAAAAAAAAAA!!
!!!!"

Bangs herself on her head. Fists clenched. Pulls her own hair.

"NOOOOOOOOOOOOOOOOOOOOOOOOOOOOOOOOOO
OOOOO!!!!"

Others scream as well. Eliza and The Dog.

"NOOOOOOOOOOOOOOOOOOOOOOOOOOOOOOOOOO
OOOOOO!!!"

I snort another thick rail off the workbench. I am fifteen feet tall. "*There sighs, complaints, and ululations loud resounded through the air without a star*," I say because Dante said. "*Accents of anger, words of agony, and voices high and hoarse, with sound of hands, made up a tumult that goes whirling on forever in that air forever black.*" Words float in space to be captured like fireflies. We are shaped by chaos and chance. "We are ONLY shaped by chaos and chance!" I shout. They all stop howling. The house is not silent.

"Chaos and chance and chaos and chance," Eliza says hopping down, shiver-shock for the cold cement floor. Slams a modest rail up her nose. Eyes roll back. Squeak of delight.

The Dog laughs.

Then weeps.

Then laughs again.

Then screams!

Then chuckles.

Then shouts, "All for the best!"

"ALL FOR THE BEST!"

Everyone loves the truth. Everyone loves a cage. Trapped. Forever. Dog pushes me against steel bench. Rusted and stained.

Chains hang overhead. Hand to my throat. Hard bulge tightens his blood-stained jeans. Emily looks over and grins, leering through hazy scattering lamp light.

"Use and destroy. Good night, Mr. Writer."

Dog snarls in my face, teeth red, eyes blank. Lick.

Lick back.

"*All...in good time...*" I whisper.

Music warbles at half-speed. Eliza and Emily take hands and dance in expanding pool of blood.

"End of hope sweet girls," The Dog says.

"First night was rough," Emily says to the girl. "Screaming all night. Sat on the bed and watched the doorknob rattle and twist. They knew we were new and soft and they wanted in. Pressed our feet against the dresser and hoped we were strong enough. We cried. Wanted Mommy to touch us and make it all better." Eliza weeps tenderly into Emily's shoulder. "Night stretched on. Days are bright and cheery. Nights are filled with screams." Banging and muffled scream from inside cold storage. "Remember when... remember when... Staring longingly into each other's eyes. Remember when... remember when..." Eliza cries harder. Emily rubs her back. "She was pretty" Emily says. "She was very very pretty. Not disappointed."

"You don't have to convince me," I say, Dog's hot breath against my neck. I am twenty feet tall. Drugs make cellar howl like it has a voice. It has a voice.

"Fourth night we made love, wouldn't you?" Emily says. Cellar howls. "Scared. And felt good. Passed the time."

"All the dark things," I say.

"The deep-down things," The Dog whispers. Presses hard against me. I can smell him, blood and sweat and dark red wine. Taste blood on his lips.

"Make love all the time," Eliza says sniffling. "Make love forever."

"Stop being her," I say. "Time is eternal. And finite."

"Stop being you," she says.

"I have a name," I announce. "It matters."

"It doesn't matter."

"It was entirely her fault!" Emily says. "I am kind! SHE is selfish!"

"Where is Emily now?" Eliza asks.

"I can take you if you come," I say. Dog grips my throat harder. My heart beats steady. Dead inside.

"Right here," Emily says. She holds the girl's face close to hers. "Right here."

"Days and nights and years bleed into one another," says The Dog. Two knives and a screwdriver, holds them to my face with one hand like metal claws. "And they bleed and bleed. Always bleeding. Coming and bleeding. Look at us! Look at us! Bleed and bleed and always bleeding."

Voices bleed. All bleed together.

"Every choice is a prison. Every prison is a choice."

"Someone dreams it. Someone builds it. Someone dwells inside it."

"Why would we choose a cage?"

"Safer than not choosing a cage."

Emily holds the girl's face in her hands. Tears burning cheeks and palms. "You and me?" Emily says. "Forever? The circle room awaits. Perfect symmetry."

"Baby-blanket soft," girl sniffles.

"Escape," I say.

"ESCAPE IS ITS OWN PRISON!!!" Dog howls.

"You can taste the rot and death. Sob and retch," Emily says.

"You retch, you wretch!" Dog snarls.

Cold storage pounds. Muffled wails.

"You have a job to do. Emily," I say. "Do your goddamn job. Face the death."

"Dead soles of cold feet...wide empty eyes—"

"FACE THE DEATH!"

Emily kisses Eliza, hard and long, tears pouring down the girl's face.

"Say it," Emily says. "Tell me you love me."

"I love you, Emily. I love you."

"Say you're my girl."

"I'm your girl. I will always be your girl." Kiss. Tender. Soft. "*I'm sorry.*"

Eliza picks cellar door key from pocket of Emily's silk night robe. Steps back, sobbing.

"What are you doing?!" Emily gasps, face blanching sick-white, stained and blotchy, running mascara. "Stop it!"

"Body is currency," The Dog says. Walks over and kisses Emily as well, smearing blood on her lips. Drops all three weapons in front of her. "Only the best for your sweet girl."

Eliza takes my left hand. Dog takes my right. Nuzzles damaged face against my neck. Blood on my throat. "Billie waits for you," I whisper to him. He nods, vague recognition.

"NO!" Emily screams.

"Told you we were acquainted," I say to her.

"YOU CAN'T LEAVE ME HERE ALONE!"

"There are others here for your company upstairs. Many and few."

"YOU CAN'T LEAVE ME!"

"And down here as well."

"PLEASE!"

"Make your peace with this."

"YOU CAN'T!"

"Saw my opportunity and grabbed it." I say. "Wouldn't you?"

"You can't be serious!"

"I can be serious."

"This is MY story!"

"Do not look back," I tell Eliza and The Dog. "You'll turn to salt."

"Please don't!" Emily cries.

"Don't look back at her," I say. "You'll turn to stone."

"I'll do better!" she pleads. "I promise!"

"She'll suck you...all the way back down."

"Down and down and down-and-down-and-down…" Eliza says, sniffling.

Emily screams, "I don't want to be one of your characters!!!"

Snatches knife from the floor and slashes at me. Release The Dog's hand, block with my right forearm. Emily cuts me wide open. Shockwave of pain streaks up and down my arm. Drugs make me see pain in pulsing waves in the air. With left hand I grab her face and squeeze, pushing cartilage from her nose into her skull with my palm. She screams. Drops knife to the floor. Like liquid ruby, the puddle advances, knife goes splat. Squeeze harder. Her face scrunches, red as a ripe tomato. Kind of adorable. Hot tears spill from her eyes, blood drips from her nose, she collapses to her knees. On the floor, wailing. I let go. She sobs. Dog licks her tears and blood from my palm like a good boy.

"You already are my dear," I say. Blow her a kiss. The Dog and Eliza do as well.

Eliza pads slowly up stairs and unlocks cellar door. Dog stomps up behind her. Emily blubbers in pool of blood. "*Comes a rainstorm…*" she cries, singing, "*…rubbers on your feet…*" Picks up knife, slashes her own thigh open. Shrieks. "*Get a little heat…*" Slashes the other. Shriek. Drags serrated blade across her bare chest, screaming. Angry wound opens gushing blood down mulberry silk. Knife drops, heavy bleeding. "*Nothing…can be… doooooone…*" Sings through wrenching sobs.

"Some sunny day," I say. Turn to leave, then turn back to look at her one last time. I do not turn to stone.

Emily curls up on the floor, fetal, woozy from pain and blood loss. Rolls to her back, holding knife above her face. Jabs forehead. Winces and squeaks. Jabs forehead again.

"Carve it off," she groans, gasping. "Carve it all off." Readies knife to carve off her face in strips. Pounding from inside cold storage in back. Muffled shouting.

"You should get that door, Emily," I say. "It's for you."

And with that, I depart.

His Tender Mouth

[Pages fed through a crack in the glass]

"It is curious," she said finally.

"Is it?"

"You feel you have spent time with me before. But I've never met you until now."

"That's precisely how I feel whenever someone reads me."

"But that's just a constructed version of you. And not an honest one."

"You echo me."

"Fair enough."

"How are you getting on?"

"There is a certain serenity in hopelessness."

"That's not something you'd want to get used to."

"You would be amazed what you can get used to."

"Regrets then?"

"There was never any doubt in my mind that I'd go in some day. It was never a question of if."

"Just when."

"And six days after my fifteenth birthday seemed like as good a time as any. Seth and I were out walking in the woods, and we just so happened to come across the house."

"You remember the day?"

"For one split second, I thought twice about opening the front door, and just turning tail and running. But I was a curious girl back then." Pause. "So, whose story is this? Emily's?

Mine? Yours?"

"It's a story for everyone. It's the only story ever told. It's the story of a cage, and the people who love it." Pause. "Like you said, there is serenity in despair."

"I said *hopelessness*. Hopelessness and despair are two very different things."

"As different as fact and truth."

"Fact and truth are identical."

"Let her go, Emily."

"She left me!"

"I don't mean Emily. I mean that little girl upstairs in your bedroom. She is not your plaything."

"You don't know anything about it."

"I know what you want from her. I know what you want to make of her."

"You have no idea what I want. You could never know."

"I know grooming when I see it."

"You can't take her from me."

"You're right, I can't. I'm just writing a book."

"Fuck you! That's not important!" Pause. "You can't take her from me. *She is me.*"

"She is not you. Surely you realize that. She's not Emily either."

"Close enough. Don't fancy yourself a liberator, new friend."

I lifted the cup to my lips for another sip of tea. Instant regret. My face felt hot and prickly. My stomach churned, and I felt dizzy and nauseated. I tried to tell her I thought I might be sick.

"I...I..."

"The facts won't set you free," she said.

I looked at my left hand shaking. Double vision.

"Truth... will..."

"It will," she said, inspecting my teacup. "You are right about that."

"You'll pay..." I slurred angrily. "Destroy you..."

"That took longer than it should have," she said, setting the cup down.

"You'll suffer..." I growled through my teeth, black balloons popping in my eyes. I struggled to maintain. "You fuck..."

"But you are bigger than she is."

I fell backward into the couch, still conscious, but feeling like a thousand-pound sack of gravel smothered in hot, wet gauze. I struggled to breathe. She picked up my notebook and flipped through a few pages, looking for a moment like she may cry. Her face contorted briefly into anger, then she smiled. She walked over to the door to the cellar, unlocked the door, and hung the key back on its hook. She opened the door and tossed my notebook down the stairs. "It's a treat, boy!" she said into the gaping chasm of black. "Come up and get your treat!" She walked over to the other couch, leaving the cellar door wide open, and picked up my jacket. I might have been able to move if I really struggled, but it just did not seem worth the effort. The little that I could see through ever-dimming eyes was blurry and doubled. She draped the jacket over me like a blanket, bent down and kissed me on the lips. "Goodnight, Mr. Writer. Dream good things about us." She placed her index and middle fingers on my eyelids, shutting them.

In darkness I heard the deliberate stomp of heavy boot heels against wooden stairs. *Thump... Thump... Thump...* growing louder, growing closer. Barely moving, I opened the pocket of my jacket. Nothing but my black ink pen could be felt.

Thump... Thump... Thump...

I opened my eyes just slightly to see the figure of a man standing in the cellar doorway. Shirtless. Lean and muscular. Tight, dark blue jeans stained with blood. Silver-tipped boots. He looked exactly like the man from before, the man upstairs, but wilder. Thick black hair disheveled, graying at the temples, salt and pepper stubble, smeared black mascara. He tossed a stained, gray pillowcase to the floor with a clattering *thunk*. He looked about the room, surveying the scene as if he had not seen it in a while, then reached down into the pillowcase and pulled out a length of thick steel chain.

I lay splayed across the sofa, completely still, eyes barely but slits. He smiled hungrily, stalking toward me, cowboy boots clomping against the hardwood floor. He had very pretty teeth. I did not move a muscle, save my eyes.

Thump... Thump... Thump.

He stood over me, looking down, the ends of the chain in each hand, considering his course of action. He took his time, sizing me up from top to bottom. Finally, he made his move and leaned down with the chain just above my throat.

Oh, you sweet summer children. Do you truly think you're the first to ever try to drug me?

At once, I slammed my left palm into the chain and drove it straight into his teeth with a snapping *crunch*. Both of his lips popped, spurting blood. He yelped and fell backward onto the coffee table, knocking the knives, carafe, and teacup to the floor. He attempted to reach for a knife. I punched him twice in the side of his neck, and he curled inward reflexively. Then I jabbed my right elbow into the center of his ribcage. He wheezed, swinging his chain in defense, smashing my left shoulder in the process. The pain was deep but dull, the Phenobarbital in my system keeping me at arm's length from my own reality. I grabbed him by the hair and slammed his head into the coffee table until his nose trickled blood. His eyes blackened with deep purple bruises and began to roll back in his head. Then I lifted him into a standing position and bent his right arm behind his back. He groaned in agony through gritted, red teeth, the ball and socket of his shoulder grinding. With the force of all my body weight, I drove him into the wall. *Thud.* Spurt of blood from his mouth across pale mint paint. I could feel the sweat from his naked back through my shirt. I turned him around so he could see his own pathetic, twisted visage in a mirror.

"Let's not forget ourselves, darling," I hissed in his ear, wrapping my teeth around his left earlobe, raking my incisors against hot skin and cartilage. "Fight me, and I will rip it clean from your skull."

I pulled my pen from my pocket, and with my left hand I carved into his chest the word *CRAWL* as deeply as the dull tip could manage until the hard plastic casing split halfway through the *R*, giving me a sharper edge to cut with for the rest of the job. He writhed, swallowing back the shriek that he so desperately wanted to let escape through his cracked, blood-red teeth. "That's what you do," I said. "That is all that you do. Don't forget your place." The ripped flesh of his shallow chest wound oozed, and his abdomen ran with blood and ink. "That is poison," whispered to him. "It's sure to be infected. You will need treatment soon."

He tried in vain to wriggle his bent arm free, swinging wildly with his left hand. He managed to clock me a good one on the left side of my nose as I drove him chest first through the door into the dark kitchen.

By diminishing candlelight, I bent him over the cold marble countertop face down. My right hand bent his arm back and up between his shoulder blades, my left hand planted sturdily next to his face on the counter. He snarled and tried to bite me, his busted mouth leaking and spraying blood across the countertop.

"Be good now," I said, wrenching his arm up further. "Time to be a good boy." He continued growling and snapping, but the more he twisted and squirmed, the more the agony of his shoulder bones grinding together intensified.

He stopped struggling at last, still panting through gritted red teeth. He reached under the counter with his left hand and undid his belt buckle. His dark, bloodstained jeans slid down his thighs. He reached back and unzipped my fly.

I sighed.

Okay… here we go…

I went at him with little romance. We both winced. Gritted teeth. Muscles tensed and clenched.

"Come on, sweetie," I said, tight and clipped, "don't take it so hard."

No one would be ejaculating in this exchange. This was strictly negotiation.

We sweated in near silence, angry and raw, in cold, shallow darkness as the last of the candlelight flickered out. Concentrated moonlight forced its way through the skylight above, casting a direct spot on naked, unoccupied space just to the right of us. *Far too bright. Far too much natural light.*

Finally, he relaxed and relented, licking my hand in submission. I let go of his arm and eased out and back, zipping my pants again. He lifted his and buckled his belt.

"You know what I want," I told him. "Fetch your bag of toys. I'm going in. Grab whichever you see first."

"See my opportunity," he whispered, wincing, rotating his aching shoulder and caressing his tender mouth, "and grab it."

As I returned the knives, cracked teacup, and quarter-filled carafe to the coffee table, he stuffed the steel chain and that girl's white wool scarf into the stained, gray pillowslip. He then headed, limping slightly, toward the hall and the stairway to the second story. I followed right behind.

Up the stairs we went.

At the landing, the stairway split in two directions, left and right. I followed him up the left-hand path. The sounds of screaming, rattling, and pounding grew louder the further we ascended to the top of the staircase.

The second-story corridor was a row of facing doors. Near perfect symmetry. Wailing and clatter from behind each door. *'How they scream out their affright, too much horrified to speak they can only shriek, shriek, out of tune... What a tale of terror tells, of despair...'*

Amidst the cacophony of pounding and shrieking I heard Emily's voice, unmistakable, inching ever nearer to climax. "I'm so close!" she screamed. "I'M SO CLOSE!" I also heard that young girl moaning, whatever her name was, though by the sounds she made I could not tell how fully conscious or consenting she was. With a fist to each side of the hall, The Dog knocked on seemingly random doors as he stomped, limping, gripping his pillowcase of toys in his left hand. As I walked, I heard furniture scraping across hardwood floors and doors unlatching behind me. I did not look back, lest I turn to salt or worse. '*How they clang and clash and roar, what a horror they outpour, in the bosom of the palpitating air...*'

Further as I walked, I heard a gathering of footsteps behind me. I opted to quicken my pace. At the end of the hallway, a lone door stood without match. To my right-hand side was another corridor, perpendicular, that I still have never fully seen. The Dog stood in its alcove and indicated the door with his head, then looked past me, eyes widening with concern. He shook his head and held up his hands for calm. And with that I twisted the knob and stepped inside.

It was called the circle room, for no logical reason at all. It was indeed a perfect square. Total symmetry. Black shag carpet wall to wall. Baby-blanket soft, or so I'd been told. Hard to tell under thick, heavy boots. Against opposite walls to my left and to my right stood two identical red, crushed velvet divans. The light in the room was red as well, an indiscernible shade. And there, across the room, standing in the opposing doorway, there he was.

There I was.

There you were.

We were, for the moment, indistinguishable. Every feeling, every freckle, every thought, every memory up until that moment identical in every way. We were the same man. But we were not mirrors of one another. Each of us had bruising on the left side of his face, weathered, worn hard and weary, and a small crust of coagulated blood around his left nostril. I noticed, in that moment, that I could only breathe through my right. I don't know if you noticed that just then as well. I will never know.

We stood and stared in the circle room. Stared into each other's dull, gray eyes. Were they hazel once? They were hazel once. Upon a time. Dark rings. Exhausted and lost. I cannot even pretend that you were pretty. If ever we were, those days had passed. You stared at me, and I stared at you, through stringy, sweat-drenched hair speckled with another man's blood. In silence. We knew what was coming. We knew what came next. It was to be what had been planned.

I was just about to say, "Let's leave," and you said, "Let's leave." And in that brief moment, we were suddenly, slightly different people. You were slightly faster by the chaos of chance. And so, chaos and chance would then choose our fate. Our fates, come what may. Come what may, I would never see you again.

We stepped out into an empty, silent corridor. No screams. No bangs. No rattling knobs. Not a peep, not a squeak, not a soul to be seen. I was to your right, where there was no perpendicular hallway, but by chance, perchance, more hands must have found me than you.

Beat for beat, punch for punch, it was very like a novel I had written years ago, a murder mystery set in DC and Wheeling, West Virginia. In a flash, my arms, head, and chest were all restrained as I fought and lost against unseen captors. I tried to yell, but a strong arm in a flannel sleeve muffled my voice. I wasn't like the protagonist of my novel, though, taken by surprise and double-crossed by a duplicitous dame. I knew this was coming, for me or for you. I knew the plan good and well. It could have been either of us, yet chaos chose me. But still I fought, from instinct, much like a drowning man would.

I struggled to get free as my arms were tied tightly in front of me. The raw hemp rope burned against my wrists, sawing through my skin, blood dripping hot down my fingers. Foam rubber ball gag forced into my mouth, secured by that girl's white wool scarf. Hard, tight, triple knotted. All went full dark as my head was enveloped in the gray pillowcase. I swung my head back, hoping to make contact with the bridge of a nose. A sickening crunch told me of my success, the gurgling yelp suggested it was The Dog's nose. But God knows. All about me, indiscernible chatter, and a flurry of punching fists.

Inside the hood, I tried not to panic, but I could barely catch a breath as only my right nostril was in working order. Sweat poured from my face, and I retched bitter Phenobarbital and bile, forced back down my throat for the foam rubber ball gag. I jerked and spasmed on instinct and felt the sharp whack of what was likely a thick steel chain against the back of my skull. The pain pierced my brain, and inside the hazy dark of the hood, silent fireworks exploded all around me. It did not knock me out, but I supposed that was the intention, so I slumped my head forward, pretending unconsciousness.

Multiple hands carried me down a flight of stairs, then another, leather and rubber soles slapping loudly against hardwood. Vertical movement, forward momentum, and then another set of stairs, tight this time, as bodies, many and few, pressed into me from all sides. The air quickly grew colder, and I heard the warbling sound of Billie Holiday at half speed, dragging and warped, diminishing, growing distant, then the clunk of a large door unlocking. Through my one good nostril, I noticed a stench of death begin to intensify, then assault me at full strength all at once. I was dropped onto an ice-cold cement floor. I felt a hand on my face through the pillowcase, and I heard your voice say, "We will make a good book. I promise."

A whoosh and a clunk, and then silence. And dark. All dark.

Hours passed. No sound through the door but the distant warbling record and The Dog's clomping boots pacing about. I lay on the freezing, glazed floor, tied up and pressing on the nerves in my left shoulder in a way that shot bolts of pain through my entire body. The only air to breathe through my one good nostril was nothing but rot and death. Vomit and swallow. Vomit and swallow. I kicked at what I hoped was the door, my scream muted by the foam rubber ball gag secured by that girl's wool scarf. Whatever her name was.

I heard more voices at last, muffled and away. That young girl crying, and the older lady singing, then screaming, then singing again. I tried to yell for help, kicked against the door. But nothing. No response. Thrashing about like a dying fish on the cold storage floor caused the gray pillowslip to finally come free of my head.

Instant regret.

I stood slowly to face it on wobbling legs. Face the death. Vomit and swallow. Vomit and swallow. There they were in piles. In stacks. Backs and ribs like washboards. Wide, empty eyes. Fingers twisted into frozen hooks like talons. Faces. Some in pairs, some alone. A set of tall, blonde boys, naked, faces broken open and bodies torn apart. A bearded man, skull caved in. Women and men and boys and girls cold and dark and all death. Beyond the rows of bodies, in the top right corner of the room was a cracked safety window, with just more cold and dark beyond it.

Death comes soon for everybody. For every single one. It comes in heaps and piles.

Wrists bound, I clawed fruitlessly at the white wool scarf tied hard and tight around my mouth, and triple-knotted behind my head. Wrists bound, I cannot work the knot. Wrists bound, I slammed against the cold storage door, hollering to whomever might hear. Trying not to panic. Trying to get enough air into my lungs. No reply. Nothing. I heard more voices. I heard The Dog. I heard Emily. I heard you spouting Dante and everybody howling. I heard that girl crying out in ecstasy, coming hard. No one heard me screaming for help.

* * *

Hours passed; voices intensified. A fight. Shouting, laughing then crying, then laughing, then "ALL FOR THE BEST!" More voices. I heard someone say, "cold storage," and I yelled and threw my body against the door. No response. I did again, to no avail.

I heard Emily scream, "WHAT ARE YOU DOING?! YOU CAN'T LEAVE ME HERE ALONE! I AM NOT ONE OF YOUR CHARACTERS!!!" I heard you shout out in pain, then Emily wailed and sobbed. Boots clomped up the stairs, and I slammed my body against the door once again, my shoulder throbbing. My right nostril swelling closed. I was sure to suffocate. I panicked, which forced me to take harder breaths, which made the swelling worse. Emily began to sing, then shriek. Then sing, then shriek. "I'll carve it all off!" she wailed, and I tried to call out to her, pounding my forehead against the thick storage door. Blood and a dull ache. I heard your voice say, "It's for you, Emily," and then your boots stomped up the stairs *Thump... Thump... Thump...*

There is no plot, there is no arc, there is no coherent script. There is only screeching noise, then agonizing silence and dark, oppressive space.

Whither Comes the Fruit

"And when…IgrowAAAAAAAAAAAAAA!!!…too old to dream… AAAAAAAA!!!… I'll climb… inside a hole AAAAAAAAAAA!!!… and sleep…"

I wasn't sure she would make it. I heard her crawling across the cellar floor, singing, voice fading ever fainter as she crawled. *Come on, come on, come on…* It was reaching the point that I could simply not breathe at all, my right nostril swelling almost entirely shut.

"And w-…. wuh… when… I rise again… It'll be as s-s-s-something looow… something… slow… at the left hand… of… Lucifer…"

My blood starved for oxygen, and the fear of suffocation grew worse as the first light of morning broke outside, dull but visible through the cracked security glass.

Finally, I heard the handle on the storage door *clunk*, and the door creaked open. I found her in a mulberry silk slip dangling from the door handle, drenched mostly though not exclusively in her own blood, overjoyed to see me, if woozy. Blood dripped from her nose and streaked down her face where she had gouged at herself with a serrated knife, and oozed heavily from the lacerations on her thighs and across her chest.

"Hi!" Emily said to me, her voice cracked and faltering. "Yes, hi! How are you?"

She tried to stand and fell into me. I lifted her up, cradling her in my arms, my wrists still bound, my lungs burning for new air. Limp, she wrapped her arms around my neck, and I carried her. As quickly as I could I followed the trail of red she had left in her crawling wake, back to the main room of the cellar. There I saw a body wrapped in a stained quilt, and the corpse of the older lady in an ever-expanding crimson pond of her own making. I laid Emily on her back across a wooden workbench like a sacrifice, then snatched one of the serrated knives from the floor. I spotted my notebook there as well, heavily damaged with bloodstains, but still salvageable [*in fact, many of the pages you have been receiving thus far*]. I brought the knife to Emily and, weakly, and with little urgency, she sawed through the raw hemp binding on my wrists.

Come on! Come on! COME ON!!!

Once finally free of the ropes, I unknotted the wool scarf from behind my head and ripped it off my face, then quickly pulled the foam rubber ball gag out of my mouth. I gasped, hard and pained, breathing in great belts of cold, stagnant cellar air, filling my desperate lungs with its putrescence. Looking about the space, I saw bottles of wine, powders and pills and gel caplets, and razor blades. In a ceramic bowl, I spotted morphine gel caps of varying strengths and doses. I placed two in Emily's mouth and held a bottle of white wine to her lips to wash them down. She gulped and coughed, wincing from the pain of the cough, which likely opened her wounds even wider. I then dropped two thicker doses down my own throat.

"Shunna done thisss to m'self..." Emily slurred, indicating her bleeding, lacerated body, her skin draining to a sickly white. "Oooopsss. Was gunn carve my own face offff too. Never wunn see her again..."

"It's fine, Miss Conlin. It's fine."

Above the workbench in a series of rusted metal cabinets I found The Dog's stash. Chemicals and tinctures, ointments and sutures, ball gags and cock rings and leather wrist restraints. All manner of business for those brought all the way down to take it hard, including aftercare.

"Would you like summ tea?" Emily slurred, giggling. "Careful, iss hot."

I nodded and poured rubbing alcohol and hydrogen peroxide into all three of her larger wounds. She shrieked and thrashed in agony. I pinned her to the table, and she lay moaning and convulsing. She continued to whimper and squeak as I dabbed the gouges on her forehead with the antiseptic. "Careful," I said. "It's hot."

She groaned softly but did not fight me as I closed her lacerations carefully and tightly with my fingertips, and sealed them up with liquid bandage. I then wrapped each in the cleanest gauze I could find. I knew we were staring down the barrel of weeks and weeks of cleaning and wound care. *There is always time. Time enough.* She was sure to have deep, lifelong scars from then on.

I scooped what remained of the squished fruit from the ceramic bowls into her mouth for a bit of glucose to the system. She sucked at my fingers like a starving calf. I hoped to find some leafy greens in the vegetable crisper upstairs to accelerate (or at least assist) in her blood production. Either way, the next several weeks of recovery were sure to be subdued and mellow. Low on hot action. Heavy on stillness and silence. *Probably bring the wine upstairs. Maybe a few other things also.*

"This is quiet," she whispered, delirious, lightly caressing my cheek with the fingertips of her left hand. "This is private down here. We can talk. We can talk in private. Get...get your notebook. It's over there in the blood. We have a book to write. You and me. A book to write forever. And ever."

'A writer is a writer' said Edwidge Danticat, 'even when there's no hope...'

"It's fine, Miss Conlin. It's fine."

I lifted her gingerly, cradling her in my arms once again. She nestled her head into the crook of my shoulder and draped her arms loosely around my neck. I carried her, cold and wet, shivering and white, over to the stairs, careful not to slip on the slick cement.

"So, I hate to be drab right from the get-go," she whispered as I carried her up the narrow cellar staircase, "but there are a few things we need to knock out before we really get cracking on this project…"

"It's fine, Miss Conlin. It's fine."

I sighed heavily, thinking about the myriad tasks ahead of me. After cleaning her up, helping her change her clothes, getting some more morphine down her throat, then getting her settled for some well-needed rest, I knew that I would have to come back down again. Down and down and down and down and down. All the way down. To stack the new bodies in cold storage, to scrub the cellar floor, to clean up the work area thoroughly. It was to be quite the undertaking. *This is your mess, you stupid fucking twat. But fuck it, I guess I will mop it up for you.* There is always time. Time enough. All in good time.

"Well, see…" Emily said as I carried her, still woozy and delirious, "this house is different. People, when they talk at all about it at all, say it should be bulldozed. Claim it's an eyesore. But that never happens. And it's not like it's out in the open or anything. It is pretty far back in the brambles and briars. Nobody *ever* comes in. Nobody I ever saw. We would hear stories of people who had. Sometimes strangers in town on a dare or something. They would roll into town to check it out. Then they would…vanish."

Notes from Under the Ground

'And in conclusion, gentleman, the best thing to do is nothing! The best thing is conscious inertia! And so hurrah for the underground!'

I spend a lot of time down here these days. You get used to the fragrance (which can be masked by kerosene and small fires), and it is quiet, save the warbling drag of the hand-cranked phonograph. I considered bringing the other one down here, the one from the parlor, but I like this one better. It is damaged. I like that it's damaged. I have to admit that I am a little tired of these two albums, but I'm writing my own music now these days, so, like, that's all good. And whatnot.

If for the moment you see the real me
If for the moment you see the real me televised
Tell it high, tell it high
I belong under the ground
I belong under the ground
where the sun is down
muffled by screaming eyes
Who'll kill it?
Who'll burn it?
Who'll ban its healing lies?
Who'll lock me?
Who block me?
Who'll stop me from stealing lives?

The book I'm writing these days and feeding through a crack in the glass page by blood-stained page is not one that I am creating with a tremendous amount of care or consideration. It just isn't. I will leave that up to you. '*I don't want to restrict myself in any way by editing my notes. I will not attempt any order or method. I will write down whatever comes to mind. As for readers, I will never have any.*' That is, of course, presuming that you are actually using these pages. Perhaps you are not. I'll never know, and it is truly fine with me either way.

The plot, in a nutshell, concerns a young woman named Emily Conlin who claims to have been trapped for nearly twenty years in a house occupied by another Emily Conlin, and several other people also accompanied by *others* of themselves. Because "only one enters and only one leaves," everyone within the house is trapped unless they are willing to kill or double-cross their other, or their other is willing to do so. Some people do just that. Some fall madly in love with their other, but most simply attempt to survive within the confines of the house, recreating some semblance of civilization, albeit a strictly contained one. Within the constructed culture of the house, identities are created and destroyed, rules are created (and violated), and order constantly teeters on the edge of chaos and violence.

After her escape, Emily hires a handsome, charming, wildly successful and not at all past-his-prime author to ghostwrite her story, through the lens of her experience, which he finds somewhat lacking. The writer, completely sober of course, decides to enter the house himself to witness firsthand the absurd horrors contained therein, and meet the other Emily, who is now trapped forever in the house. What he finds is a far more overtly domineering and manipulative Emily than the one he had met on the outside. Other folks who have devolved into grotesque caricatures of acceptable human behavior (including a fairly recent arrival – a very young woman who seemingly has no other self within the house, and is apparently "trapped" there entirely of her own accord). Though the writer claims to be strictly an impartial observer within the house, he quickly becomes an agent of disruption. He viciously murders one of the inhabitants with no pause or remorse, and just as viciously "forces liberation" [Emily's wording] on another, before being driven down into the cellar, where this tableau of the damned is reduced to grunts, screams, and context-free fragments of mis-remembered conversation, until the entire narrative collapses and circles back again [at least that's what the fuck it sounded like through the door of the cold storage room].

'Why, actually, do I want to write at all? If not for an audience then couldn't I simply go over everything just in my mind, without putting it on paper? I might get some relief from writing it all down.'

Knowing that she will never escape the confined space she inhabits, the main character of *The Duplication House** re-constructs herself as a tyrant and a predator, enduring the passage of time by waiting for a new naïf to walk through the door whom she can befriend, ensnare, and possess. [*The Duplication House* is a placeholder title, and at best an imprecise one. You can name it whatever you like.] I feel as though I have captured Emily fairly well in my version, though as you know, there is a lot about her that just does not translate to the page. Due to the inherent limitations of language, I am simply incapable of describing many of the attributes and qualities she possesses. At least right now. Maybe you have done better in your version. God knows as The Dog knows, I'll never see it.

'Though I have said that I envy the normal man to the point of the bitterest gall, yet, under the conditions in which I see him, I do not want to be one.'

A split, and not terribly smooth, presentation of mockery and sympathy runs with relative consistency through *The Duplication House** as it does in the actual house here, as does also the perpetual interchange of boredom and carnage. Around these parts, I see folks suffering through their imprisonment by constructing and deconstructing their very conceptions of themselves, in pairs and alone. Sometimes fatally. Gotta pass the time somehow, right?

I certainly have no investment in alleviating their suffering. All things being equal (and they are) I am perfectly happy contributing to it. The only thing that matters is the story. That's all I care about. That is all I have ever cared about.

If for the moment you see the real me
If for the moment you see the real me paralyzed
buried with my pair of lies...
I belong under the ground
I belong under the ground
where the sound is drowned out
by the scream of stolen eyes
Who'll kill it?
Who'll burn it?
Who'll ban its healing lies?
Who'll lock me?
Who block me?
Who'll stop me from stealing lives?

Finally, the reader will see this amoral commitment to the narrative *über alles* in the final moments where the author Emily had hired to tell her story is found beaten, bound and gagged, locked in the cold storage with all the other corpses. That he and his other were perfectly willing to literally sacrifice him with no hesitation and little regard for the consequences in order to complete the book is not the most subtle commentary on the writing process either of us could have made, but it is certainly apt. (*'Suppose I had shut YOU up for forty years without a thing to do, then came to you, in your underground hole, to see what had become of you'*). Like I said, only the story matters. Nothing else. Not a thing else.

I'll write more later. Be on the lookout for more pages soon. I'm going upstairs for a bit. As brother Fyodor said, *'To the devil with the underground.'*

In every man's memory, there are things he won't reveal to others, except, perhaps to friends. And there are things he won't reveal even to friends, only, perhaps, to himself, and then, too, in secret. And finally, there are things there are things he is afraid to reveal even to himself...But now, precisely now, when I have not only recalled them but decided to write them down, I want to test whether it's possible to be entirely frank at least with oneself and dare to face the whole truth. I have hundreds of such memories; but at times one will come up out of the hundreds and oppress me —Dostoevsky.

No guidance at all about how the piece should be properly presented. It is nothing but fragments of words, phrases and ideas that whisper and scream in anguish and torment about drugs, about sex, about abuse from without and within, about the fear of, and a longing for, death.

Whatever. It's all the same.

I think about you often. I suspect that I think about you more than you think about me. I suspect that I think about you more than you think about you. Understand: I am not mad. I'm not guilty of the sin of anger, only the crime of curiosity. When I imagine you, you look almost exactly like me, with just some small, nearly intangible differences. Perhaps it's the slight increase in sun exposure. Very slight, I'm assuming. Perhaps it is your mistaken idea that you are the one of us who is free.

> Though few at the time could have guessed that *Waiting for Godot* would resonate so strongly with San Quentin's inmate audience, in hindsight it is not difficult to imagine how this material might speak clearly to the experience of a prisoner, nor is it difficult to see how *Waiting for Godot* might have resonated with the denizens

of the besieged Sarajevo of 1993 and flood-ravished New Orleans of 2004. The context-specific resonance of *Waiting for Godot* also illustrates the enduring power of absurdist art to speak to a variety of complex human circumstances. Absurdism, after all, is that unruly branch of philosophy that states all "meaning" is thin fabrication and delusion, and life is endless chaos. Because it is human nature to want to construct meaning, that chaos is unsettling in a primal way. Absurdism insists that we confront the reality of our own insignificance, then mocks our desire to make sense of it. From a socio-political perspective, however, the Theatre of the Absurd has the capacity to make us question the systems of oppression that are themselves man-made fabrications (prison, slavery, etc.) In doing so, it can shed light on what Foucault has described as the modern "disindividualiz[ation]" of "power" that does not manifest itself as a single oppressive entity, but instead "a certain concert-ed distribution of bodies, surfaces, lights, gazes" bespeaks the Theatre of the Absurd's representation of "an arrangement whose internal mechanism produce the relation in which individuals are caught up" (*Discipline and Punish* 202). Moreover, just as Foucault illustrates how the systems of power within society have long utilized theatrical elements to cow the populace, so, too, do we see absurdist playwrights like Samuel Beckett re-appropriate those same theatrical conceits to mock the artificiality of those oppressive power systems. This mockery can be equally as risible as it is disturbing, often at the same time. It is as hilarious as a Marx Brothers routine, and as nightmarish as Artaud's *The Spurt of Blood*. As legless old Nell from Beckett's *Endgame* announces from within her garbage can, "Nothing is funnier than unhappiness" (14).

I imagine you not in physical, real-life terms, but on film, on an Arriflex 35BL. Like a movie, or a show, like the ones I never sold. (Maybe you have at long last.) Sometimes it is 16mm instead, depending on if the shot is wide or tight, interior or exterior (such options!). Sometimes I imagine you on a stage, but still on film, distressed and overexposed, giving exposition to an audience I never see. I suspect you don't see them either.

It's been a long way down
A long way down
And we've still got miles to fall
And when we say that we could take it
Who quite knew that we'd take it all?

It is easy to see Beckett's repeated use of the "crippled tyrant" archetype like Pozzo (*Godot*) and Hamm (*Endgame*), and these tyrants' relationship to their exhausted and tormented clown-slaves (Lucky and Clov, respectively) as being direct commentary on that same lopsided power construct. As shown within their respective plays, Pozzo and Hamm's authority is baseless, and their punishments arbitrary. Lucky and Clov could easily overpower them, and yet they never do. (Clov threatens to leave, though it is an empty gesture, as he would have nowhere to go if he did). Their roles within the relationship are already firmly in place and go unquestioned. This lopsided power dynamic is as frustrating as it is grimly comical.

Well, white lines are fine when the money's on time
But jackets and crosses will do
So just rage at the sun
Get the damn deal done
And give the devil hers too

The film that I watch is about a man who justifiably dwells on his failures. Endlessly. A man who is not very old. A man who looks older than he is. A man with ashen eyes and damaged organs. A man who is constantly looking ahead to the next endeavor, knowing that it is likely destined to go south, deep or otherwise. A man who only looks back to inquire as to how far he has fallen. The answer is consistently "all the way down," but there is still yet far to fall.

Beckett's perceived subversion of the power of tyrants (and subsequent championing of the downtrodden) is more ambiguous than a Foucauldian read of his writings might claim. Just as Foucault and Goffman illustrate that sympathy or aid to the condemned was discouraged in 17th and 18th century public punishment (by both a show of force and an invitation to "join in the fun" of mockery and abuse), so too are we as Beckett's audience seemingly discouraged from pitying Clov and Lucky due to their grotesque unpleasantness. We are called upon to look down on them with contempt and revulsion, when in actuality they are our closest surrogates within these absurd environments. *Endgame*'s Clov and *Godot*'s Lucky have no agency; they are servants precisely because that is how they are written. Furthermore, Hamm and Pozzo have no agency either for precisely the same reason; they are tyrants on the page, and can only be tyrants on the stage.

It's been a long, slow grind
A long, slow grind
And we're still down a key or two
And as we grind this corn or grind this ax
We'll grind these fuckers for you

We see Beckett highlighting, and mocking, the idea of the Foucault's Panopticon in *Endgame*, wherein the two symmetrical windows that seem to loom over Hamm and Clov (as well as the two legless people in the ashcans) serve as the unblinking eyes of the power system. Yet, as Clov repeatedly tells us, they look out across nothing but oblivion. Moreover, we see Beckett present a toppling, albeit an accidental one, of the crippled tyrant in the second act of *Waiting for Godot*. When the now mute Lucky falls down, as he is wont to do, he yanks Pozzo to the ground with him. Pozzo, who like *Endgame's* Hamm is now blind, screams pitifully for help as Vladimir (the second of *Godot's* two hobo-clowns) remarks, "at this moment of time, all mankind is us whether we like it or not" (Act II). Vladimir and his partner Estragon attempt to lift up Pozzo and Lucky, and they all tumble down in a tangled heap. Everyone is hurt, no one has been helped. As it should be.

Well, white lines are fine when the money's on time
But jackets and crosses are too
So just rage at the sun
Get the damn deal done

And give the devil her due

The movie that I watch is about a man who is always alone, and is yet a complete and utter fraud when he writes about loneliness. Because he truly does not know how it feels. He has never felt lonely a day in his life. He has witnessed people cry, kill, and die over loneliness, and he cannot relate. But no matter. He often writes about genuine human emotions which he has never actually felt. He is an adept faker, a skilled and gifted liar. And really, at the end of the day, isn't that better anyway?

Cuz we've been smokin'
And poppin'
And sniffin'
And droppin'
And coppin' a brand new score
And now that we took just a bit too much
All we need's just a little more

Resistance to the expectation of satisfying narrative resolution, as we see in the stage work of Genet and Beckett, is a hallmark of absurdist theatre. By eschewing the expectations of the traditional narrative arc, the Theatre of the Absurd creates and perpetuates an unresolved tension within the audience. Beckett's Gogo and Didi wait for Godot every day, yet he never arrives. Genet's maids and crooks claw and fight to get above their station, but the effort is ultimately for nothing. Real life, after all, is inherently unsatisfying, and an individual's life is never resolved; it simply ends. Absurdist writers like Beckett and Genet hold up a cracked mirror to society and force us to look at ourselves at our most broken and ridiculous—self-centered, violent, and random in both word and deed.

Well, white lines are fine when the money's on time
But jackets and crosses will do
So just rage at the sun
Get the damn deal done
And give the devil hers too

The flicker I watch in my mind is about a man who, truthfully, honestly, should probably end his own life. Yet, he never will. Not because he has any drive to continue on, or desire to do great work, or even a particular will to live, but because if by some absurd longshot there is an afterlife, he is genuinely afraid that it will be boring. I wish I could tell him that there is, and it is. It very much is. But he will never hear me. Either way, continue to exist he will. All for the best (and who would receive my pages otherwise?). Besides, were he to cease to be, many people would miss him. Many people he will never miss in return.

It's been a long way down
A long way down
And we've still got miles to fall
And when we say Good golly (Good golly) miss Molly
Don't you know she sure like to ball

Language ceases to be language devoid of context, and observation does not exist in a vacuum. Just as the inmates at San Quentin in 1957 watched, and evaluated, *Waiting for Godot* through the lens of their own context, so too, do we all, whether we mean to or not. And as that context shifts, so will our perception and appraisal of the information we absorb. So too will our recognition of what the work is saying about the human experience, and whether or not we find it truthful. In art, in language, in life, context is all.

Well, white lines are fine when the money's on time
But jackets and crosses are too
So just rage at the sun
Get the damn deal done
And give the devil her due

Just as the broader components of the Narcissus and Echo myths lend themselves well to an absurdist interpretation, so too does the story of Orpheus and Eurydice, with its inherent "cruelty and terror," fit well with an Artaudian presentation. Within most canonical versions of this narrative, the musician Orpheus plays so beautifully that his music can calm Cerberus, the savage, three-headed guard dog of Hades, and so mournfully that all the nymphs of the forest will weep. Even the hardened heart of Hades himself can be softened by the music of Orpheus. So, when Eurydice, Orpheus's beautiful wife, is killed by a snake and dragged down to Hades, Orpheus descends after her. Because he is moved by Orpheus's music, Hades allows Orpheus to take Eurydice back to the land of the living, but only if he can avoid looking back at her before they have crossed the threshold of the Upperworld. Because Orpheus is incapable of resisting the urge to look back at her, Eurydice is dragged back to Hades at the last moment, doomed to dwell there forever. I don't care who you are, that is funny as hell. As funny as Hell is.

Cuz we've been smokin'
And poppin'

And sniffin'
And droppin'
And coppin' a brand new score
And now that we took just a bit too much
All we need's just a little more

Though most myths involving Hades present him as more passively unfeeling than overtly malicious, narratives surrounding Hades (and his namesake land of the Underworld) are rife with rape, death, torment and anguish, pain and grotesquerie. The myths of Orpheus in particular seem suited to a presentation within the Theatre of Cruelty, given the juxtaposition of hauntingly beautiful music and screams of eternal torment. Also, in a very Artaudian fashion, these myths entirely eschew any traditional Judeo-Christian conceptions of morality, despite a modern audience's likely association of Hades with biblical notions of Hell and Satan. The story of Orpheus and Eurydice is primal to its core, with little *a priori* moral considerations, let alone moral lessons. If I were ever to write another novel, I think it would have a three-act structure with subtle shifts in genre from one to the next. Throughout the three acts, the small cast of characters would negotiate the various power dynamics among them, often switching characteristics on a dime and interchangeably adopting the personae of the mythic characters Echo, Narcissus, Eurydice, Orpheus, Hades, and even Cerberus. Though it might as a whole ultimately follow a recognizable (if circular) narrative structure, the presentation of that narrative as it moves through the stylistic trappings of different storytelling forms might disrupt the audience's expectations of linear narrative. Expectations of audience sympathies could also be disrupted as characters shift from one personality type to another, and the lines blur between victim and aggressor, oppressor and oppressed. That would be pretty cool. I don't think I'm going to do it, though.

Well, white lines are fine when the money's on time
But jackets and crosses will do
So just rage at the sun
Get the damn deal done
And give the devil hers too

Do you ever think about all of the friends that you have, all the friends and lovers you have had over the years? I do. I have a lot of time to think these days. Be honest: have you actually been making friends all this time? Have you truly been building relationships? Or have you simply been collecting characters? Are people actually *people* to you, or are they just random collections of quirks, types, and traits? Do you think your friends would still be your friends if they knew the truth about you? How do you think they would feel if they ever found out who you truly are? If they knew what you truly are? If they ever found out about all of the things that you have done? All of the things that no one (who is still alive) knows about? I know about them, of course. But, of course, I shan't tell.

I taste the setting sun and faced the final run.
The last stop until I'm done.
Heart beats way too fast.
I was never meant to last, and now
my bones here weigh a ton.
Can't come down when you're flying quite this high,
drunk on the moonlight and drowning in the sky.

Serious question: why do you take all of those pills? What are they for? What do they do? Do you even remember anymore? I take different pills now. I wonder if that means I am now different from you. Our chemical make-up differs now. Our meat and gristle have been altered, likely changed in a substantial fashion. And we are all just meat and gristle anyway. It happens.

I had a dream last night
and lost every single fight.
This time there is just no getting right.
I want it over now.
But this is it, somehow.
This crime will keep my fists forever tight.
Can't come down when you're flying quite this high,
drunk on the moonlight,
and drowning in the sky.

As I look out this parlor window into the thick of the woods, I see the snow is falling. *'Yesterday it snowed too, and the day before.'* I have no particular feelings about snow. I don't recall sledding or playing in the snow as a child. Or if I do recall the activity itself, I don't recall enjoying it, or not enjoying it, for that matter. Emily does. She is down the hall right now weeping, staring longingly out the window, missing the feel of the snow on her face. She misses playing with her friends on the sledding hill, throwing snowballs, and making snowmen, tracing snow angels on the ground. She misses warming up with a steaming mug of hot cocoa by the crackling fire, singing hillbilly lullabies in her momma's lap until the wee hours. I cannot relate in the slightest. And I must express some relief for that, as she appears to be in tremendous pain for the memories. Scarcely seems worth it to me.

Had a dream last night and faced the setting sun.

This time there is no getting done.
I want it over now. I want it all.
Somehow, my shadow weighs a ton.
Can't come down when you're flying quite this high,
drunk on the moonlight,
and drowning
in the sky.

Emily *misses* a lot. Constantly. She thinks back wistfully on the past, on people and events that mattered for some reason. She remembers far too much. She is tormented by her memories, aches in her longing, torn to shreds by her desires for things that she will never, ever have. She remembers her first skinned knee, her first crush, her first broken bone, her first broken promise, her first broken heart. Why would one remember their first crush? Why remember anything? Why remember at all? "I remember the snow," she says, sniffling, gliding her tear-damp fingertips down the cold glass of the living room window. "I remember everything precisely as it was." So, then, I suppose, *'let this be a tale on the occasion of wet snow.'*

Eternal, and Finite

We do okay...we do okay...

Emily's recovery took a bit longer than I had hoped it would, including two rounds of particularly nasty infections. Multiple nights of high fever dreams and screaming night terrors were enjoyed by all. But she came around eventually. Her scars are deep and substantial. But now, at last, overall, her body is in okay enough shape. Her mind, perhaps, is another matter entirely. But what constitutes sane within these walls is a fluid and subjective notion anyway.

I am grateful that you left the bags behind when you departed. I have added most of the textbooks to the parlor bookshelves, replacing some of the worst offenders that had previously occupied space there. They have made for decent fires on particularly cold nights. I have also discovered in an attic space some broken and forgotten musical instruments I have taken to refurbishing. Like I said some pages ago, after all this time, I am finally writing music again. No one will ever hear it, of course, but who needs an audience anyhow. Perhaps I'll write out some notations and chord progressions for you at some point. Maybe you can do something with them. ~~It was nearly as if I found them because I wanted to find them without realizing that I did. As if the house knew I wanted them. As the house divides, the house provides. (That's a line. Use it if you want.)~~

I am curious to know if you ever got the degree, if it made any difference to your life, if you ever found any satisfaction. At all. I have often wondered if you ever completed your version of the book, this book, and if you've included any of the pages I have been feeding through the crack in the glass all this time (These are my *Letters from the Underworld*, which is what that novel is *actually* called). I have had to rearrange the cold storage room several times now—which is, in a word, *traumatizing*—and yet even still, access to the window continues to be a struggle. We may have to make some drastic changes before too long. Nevertheless, Emily and I have decided to keep writing this book, possibly forever. And as long as I continue to see your silhouette on the other side of the security glass, I will continue to feed pages through it. (Well… I am assuming that it's you out there. I suppose I will never truly know.)

I have wondered if Aunt Billie ever got her son back, and if there was anything left of him to salvage. She lost a kid and got a creature in return. I have long presumed that he probably would not be able to maintain terribly well outside of the house, and would likely find himself in very confined spaces again in no short amount of time. Time enough. I would be happy to be proven wrong, however. Even if I'm not, though, perhaps that's not so bad, anyway. Jean Genet always loved prison, after all. It was his favorite place to be. He found comfort in that confined space. "Good and proper screwing in there, too," Emily says. Who am I to argue?

She no longer speaks of it much, but I know Emily still misses that red-haired girl, whatever her name was. Green Eyes. I have wondered about her too, and thought that there might be myriad potential stories there if you were inclined to pursue them. And if she was still accessible to you. Perhaps. Maybe not. Maybe there's just nothing there.

For the longest time, Emily was adamant about not bringing that girl to the circle room. She wanted so badly for the girl to *want* to stay with her, to love her by choice, to desire her freely and of her own free will. As if *anyone* gets that. As if that were an actual thing that could ever truly be (her naiveté never fails to make me laugh even now. It is kind of adorable). It wasn't until you arrived with your intention to take the girl away from her that Emily had to make the decision—two of her or none. If you had not taken her, I would likely be stuck with the former. Whatever. It's all the same to the clam.

Em and I are not always together these days, but when we are, it is as grim and sordid as you might imagine. I must admit to not being quite as versatile with the character work as she would prefer. She has lists of creative demands when we are together that are a bit of a challenge for me to complete and fulfill. Needless to say, she is a much more talented mimic than I am, and I appreciate her skills quite a bit. (Never underestimate the value of high school theatre training.) Recently I have been pressing her to try her hand at Seth. It is a bit of an abiding obsession, I must admit. She is, to put it mildly, ambivalent. "You knew him as a grown man," she protests. "I only ever knew him as a small boy. It would be *immoral*." I tell her to just use her imagination, for the imagination is devoid of morals. Morality is a human construct anyway, and not even a particularly well-designed one. She has agreed to the haircut at least, and I have to say, she looks eerily like him now. It is uncanny. She can do the voice too, younger than I prefer, but no matter. She doesn't care for the boots, though, and refuses to wear them. It is a work in progress. She barely even fights anyway. She likes the dark things deep down.

New guests to the house have been few and far between these days, and that truly is all for the best. Emily and I share a singular policy when it comes to visitors—*use twice and destroy*. You may want to pass that along to your readers, if any, lest they get overly curious about stopping by. I don't suppose that's the sort of advice that would matter to them anyway, though. Still and all, it may be worth a mention. Curiosity may not be a crime, but it is the surest path to a messy and painful conclusion. The end.

As it stands, our numbers here at the house have been dwindling quite a bit of late. Some folks have been forcibly dismissed out the front door without warning. Others are now in cold heaps and piles. You are not the only one of us whose hands are stained a permanent red (and space is already at a premium in cold storage). Those souls who remain have learned they would do well to avoid us when possible, Emily and me. Those whom I have discovered took part in grabbing me and locking me inside the cold storage room that fateful night have been taking it particularly hard. I know that it isn't fair, that they were simply tasked with a job to do. But I never claimed to be a kind person, nor even an especially good one. *"At length I would be avenged; this was a point definitively settled,"* as Poe would say. It's not just me. Emily may not be quite the monster I am, but she is no wilting flower herself. "Make you come, make you cry, make you die," Emily says. *Talents.* She is a sweet, sweet angel.

At this rate, before too long we will be down to just two here. ~~I don't know if that is what the house wants. I don't know if the house wants. It doesn't really matter to me. It doesn't matter at all anymore. We are in charge now. And we do okay.~~ We do okay.

There are so many questions I wish I could ask you. So many questions for which I will never get answers. I can't help but wonder if your version of this book is now complete, if you got paid, if Sal ever found a publisher, if people are even reading it. If Emily Outside is still a part of your life. If Seth is. I would have to think that they are not, that if they aren't already they will soon be just another *him* and *her* you can barely recall, more half-remembered faces and forgotten names you will never miss. I am, of course, trapped forever in a non-arcing narrative where they are principal players—one I will never truly see again, the other I will truly never see again. But you are not. For me, this book will never be completed. It will never end, not entirely. For you, perhaps, it has already been remaindered.

In my mind, when I see you, from a distance, you look just like me from behind. The shot tightens slowly on you, slump-shouldered and disheveled, hungover and sleep deprived in a noisy, charmless airport bar slamming overpriced Jack Daniel's and reading Dostoevsky like an asshole. Waiting for a plane. Waiting for a call. Waiting for another story you can spice up with hot action once the drafting starts. Lay on the drama; make it pop in revision. Waiting, for forward momentum.

FIN...for now

LIST OF WRITERS REFERENCED
(incomplete):

[fed through a crack in the glass]

Alighieri, Dante
Aron, Robert
Artaud, Antonin
Beckett, Samuel
Bermel, Albert
Brown, Lew
Danticat, Edwidge
Dostoevsky, Fyodor
Eshleman, Clayton
Esslin, Martin
Eyton, Frank
Foucault, Michel
Genet, Jean
Goffman, Erving
Hammerstein II, Oscar
Heyman, Edward
Harshman, Marc
Hughes, Langston
Lucas, Craig
Ovid (Publius Ovidius Naso)
Penniman, Richard
Pinsky, Robert
Poe, Edgar Allan
Sartre, Jean-Paul
Scott, Ronald Belford

Shaw, George Bernard
Silverstein, Shel
Singer, Nathan
Sour, Robert
Stoker, Bram
Tobias, Charles
Vitrac, Roger
Vonnegut, Kurt

ACKNOWLEDGMENTS

Thank you:

Derek Snow, Becca Howell, Regina Pugh, Willemien Patterson, Dylan Shelton, Serenity Fisher, Brian Tyree, Louise Smith, Diane Allerdyce, Ted Weil and the Falcon Theatre, Tom Hottle, Lance Wright, Eric Campbell and all the top-shelf folks at Down & Out Books, The Whiskey Shambles, Phantom Queen, Performance Gallery, Julie, Wolf, & Levi, and, of course, Karsten Piep (RIP).

ABOUT THE AUTHOR

NATHAN SINGER is a novelist, playwright, composer, and experimental performing artist. He is also vocalist and guitarist for award-winning "ultra-blues" band The Whiskey Shambles and the metal band Phantom Queen. His published novels are the controversial and critically-acclaimed *A Prayer for Dawn*, *Chasing the Wolf*, *In the Light of You*, *The Song in the Squall*, *Transorbital*, *Blackchurch Furnace*, and *The Duplication House*. He currently lives in Cincinnati, Ohio where he is working on a multitude of new projects.

On the following pages are a few
more great titles from the
Down & Out Books publishing family.

For a complete list of books and to
sign up for our newsletter,
go to DownAndOutBooks.com.

Waking Up the Devil
Chris Miller

Down & Out Books
August 2023
978-1-64396-325-9

A master killer is forced back into the business, and it's personal. Cade Samson has less than a day to take out his old partner before his former crime boss murders his brother. The problem is, the Feds are all over it.

Get ready for a pedal to the metal splatterfest of crime and vengeance.

"Chris Miller is one of the best kept secrets in crime fiction. But he won't be a secret anymore once readers get ahold of this masterful new offering." —Andy Rausch, author of *Hell To Pay*

Loud Water
Robby Henson

Down & Out Books
August 2023
978-1-64396-327-3

Eight years into a 15-year sentence, Crit Poppwell finally discovered something he was good at, besides destroying his family and abusing drugs. He found art. The solitary act of drawing, painting and creating brings a calmness to his chaos.

Crit returns to his hometown where his brother is the reigning crystal meth kingpin and his ex-wife wants him dead. Can Crit flush the past from his blood and bones? Or die trying?

"A brilliant noir debut with a bittersweet ending."
—Jim Winter, author of the Holland Bay series

Killin' Time in San Diego
Bouchercon Anthology 2023
Holly West, Editor

Down & Out Books
August 2023
978-1-64396-328-0

Welcome to San Diego, where the perpetual sunshine blurs the line between good and evil, and sin and redemption are two sides of the same golden coin.

Killin' Time in San Diego is a gripping anthology featuring twenty of today's best crime and mystery writers and published in conjunction with Bouchercon 2023.

From the haunted hallways of the Hotel del Coronado to the tranquil gardens of Balboa Park, from the opulent estates of La Jolla to the bustling Gaslamp Quarter, *Killin' Time in San Diego* is your ticket to the hidden side of "America's Finest City."

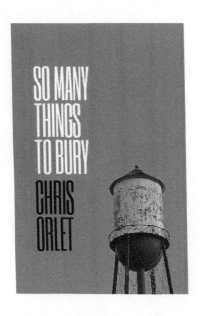

So Many Things To Bury
Chris Orlet

Down & Out Books
September 2023
978-1-64396-335-8

Al Heidorn is a working stiff, a Korean War vet and recently divorced father of three whose life is unraveling from decades of drinking and neglect. Now Al is determined to start over and put things right.

But that's easier said than done. Rather than get his life on track Al makes a tragic decision that seems likely to haunt him for the rest of his days.

Will he find redemption or will he squander the only thing that he has yet to lose—his young daughter's love and life?

Made in the USA
Columbia, SC
25 September 2024

43056906R00148